Deep Waters

"All I know is that I have a chemist who's suffered an unexplained death. I can't prove foul play but *you* might be naturally suspicious. You might think the lack of a cause of death suggests a very clever method of killing. If you did, you might want to check out his colleagues in the pharmaceutical business. After all, they're experts at making substances that interact with the human body in cunning ways."

"Mmm. Tantalizing thought," Brett agreed. "We need to look for someone with a motive and who calculated that his death would be put down to natural causes – or a complete mystery."

"Over to you," Tony proclaimed.

Look out for:

Lawless & Tilley: The Secrets of the Dead
Lawless & Tilley: Magic Eye
Malcolm Rose

The David Belbin Collection: *Avenging Angel,*
Deadly Inheritance and *Final Cut*

The Malcolm Rose Collection:
The Alibi, *Concrete Evidence* and *The Smoking Gun*

POINT CRIME

LAWLESS & TILLEY

Deep Waters

MALCOLM ROSE

SCHOLASTIC

For the students of Alsager School and St Joseph's Roman Catholic School (Chalfont St Peter)

Scholastic Children's Books
Commonwealth House, 1–19 New Oxford Street,
London WC1A 1NU, UK
a division of Scholastic Ltd
London ~ New York ~ Toronto ~ Sydney ~ Auckland

First published in the UK by Scholastic Ltd, 1997

ISBN 0 590 13372 1

Typeset by TW Typesetting, Midsomer Norton, Somerset
Printed by Cox & Wyman Ltd, Reading, Berks.

10 9 8 7 6 5 4 3 2 1

At the summit of the bleak Horsehill Tor, Detective Inspector Brett Lawless brushed the snow from a rock, sat down heavily and surveyed the Vale of Edale. Usually lush and green, the floor of the valley was now entirely white. The railway and roads were dark ribbons and the villages were grey blobs. It looked as charming and picturesque as a Christmas card. To Brett, though, the rugged valley also had an evil side. He wished that the blanket of snow could cover past horrors. Just as winter had stripped away the countryside's fertility, so he prayed that it would cloak the lingering atmosphere of death. Brett shuddered. He was remembering. He was regretting past mistakes.

The annoying and insistent chirp of his mobile phone brought him back to reality. He dragged the phone out from under several layers of clothing. "Yes?" he said, his breath forming a small cloud of condensation.

"It's me."

"Oh," he responded, recognizing the voice of his partner, Detective Sergeant Clare Tilley. Resigned to an interruption, he said, "Hi."

"Where are you?"

He hesitated, as if he did not wish to admit it, but then replied, "Walking in the Peak District."

"Isn't it a bit chilly?" asked Clare.

"Yes, it's decidedly … fresh." The tip of his nose and ears glowed bright red with the cold. "But it's beautiful," he added. "A bit eerie, as well."

"You're not at Upper Needless, are you?"

Brett frowned. Sometimes, Clare seemed to be able to read his mind. "Yeah. Up the hill by the village."

"Oh. I'm sorry to disturb—"

Cutting in, Brett said, "It's OK. What's up? Have we been summoned?"

"Yes. The Chief wants to see us. Says he's got a strange case he wants us to look into. Sunday or not. Day off or not." She added gently, "I really am sorry."

"It's OK," Brett said, getting to his feet. "I was just about ready to come back anyway," he fibbed.

"Take care," she told him. "The roads must be pretty treacherous out there."

"I'll pick you up at your place," Brett said. "Should be with you in under an hour."

The snow on the hillside was neither icy nor

slushy. It crunched and compacted under Brett's heavy boots, providing firm footing for his descent to the country lane. He had parked the car at the edge of Upper Needless. Before he opened the door, he gazed wistfully into the tiny hamlet. In the field behind the village, the farmer was driving a brand new tractor, delivering huge bales of hay to his beleaguered flock of sheep, camouflaged by their thick fleeces. A van was parked outside the grocer's shop, delivering the goods that the villagers could not grow or make for themselves. Hidden from his view, the consecrated ground behind the hall contained the new grave of his girlfriend, Zoe. A victim of his last case. Brett sighed, blinked away a tear and then unlocked his car. As he drove away, he watched Upper Needless disappear from his rear-view mirror like a half-remembered dream, like a half-remembered nightmare.

In the reception of the Sheffield police station, there was a small queue of people wearing overcoats. The Sergeant on duty had dared to remove his coat but he was paying for his bravado. He was shivering and his white fingers were hardly capable of jotting down the stream of complaints that he had to endure. In the corner, a woman was dismantling the fake Christmas tree and bagging its lacklustre decorations. She was muttering to herself, "Should've been done yesterday, this. Twelfth night's done and dusted. Just asking for bad luck." Brett swiped his warrant card through the lock on the internal door. It gave him access to the parts of the station that the public would never see, except for suspects being taken to the interview rooms or cells. With Clare, he strode down the long corridor. A large board by the common room showed the duty rotas. Inside the room, uniformed and plainclothes officers were huddled round hot drinks. On the right, the control room was buzzing with radios, telephones, computers. All calls to the police were received in the control room. The 999 calls were distinguished with red lights and alarms. Unusually, the operators were still in their coats, as if they were on the point of getting up and walking out, but the office was staffed twenty-four hours a day. From one of the smoky briefing rooms, awash with discarded plastic cups, someone shouted, "Hi, Clare!" She raised her hand in greeting but did not stop to exchange pleasantries. Alongside Brett, she headed straight for Detective Chief Superintendent Johnstone's office.

After knocking on his door, Brett and Clare breezed in. Brett had to struggle to stop himself from grinning. He had never before seen the Chief looking less than calm and professional. Now, Keith Johnstone was pacing behind his desk like a restless lion. His immaculate suit was hidden beneath a wax jacket and his big smooth hands were buried in thick gloves. He looked ready to lead a team of huskies rather than a team of police officers. It amused Brett that a little discomfort could render even the most authoritative figure comical.

"We can send a probe to Jupiter, but we can't make a heating system that doesn't break down as soon as the weather turns nasty," Keith complained. "And the engineers haven't turned up yet. Apparently we couldn't afford a service contract on the boiler so now we can't get anyone to fix it in a hurry."

"It *is* a Sunday, sir," Clare commented pointedly.

The Chief ignored her, mumbled a curse, sat down and waved the two young detectives towards seats. He pointed to his computer keyboard and grumbled, "I can't even type with these on." He held up his gloved hands. "Oh, well," he groaned, "life must go on." He pushed a briefing paper towards Brett and said, "Actually, for one Dr Colin Games, life doesn't go on. That's why I got you in. I want you to look into it. It's ideal for you, Brett. Dr Games was some sort of chemist at Pharmaceutical and Health Products."

Brett extracted a cold hand from his pocket and picked up the report. While his eyes scanned the page, he interjected, "Yes. PHP. I know them. They plough quite a bit of money into the university up the road." When Brett had taken his degree in biochemistry, some of his tutor's research had been sponsored by PHP.

"Well, Dr Games was one of PHP's major players, it seems. A key man. Now he's dead and our pathologist can't make anything of it. Baffled. No obvious cause of death. That's where you should start. Talk to Tony Rudd. He'll fill you in."

"But does *he* think it's murder?" Clare queried.

"He doesn't know what to think, to be up front about it," the Chief answered. "But you know what he's like. Tenacious. Doesn't like loose ends. If someone dies in a way that gets the better of him – well, to Tony, that's grounds for suspecting a very devious murder. He won't accept natural causes that he hasn't encountered before. He reckons he's seen it all. Of course, he won't suggest murder in so many words. He'll just provide the facts." Keith crossed his arms and hugged himself for warmth. Underneath the desk, he jiggled his legs to help his circulation. "I brought you in on a Sunday because the victim's wife's been harassing us to release the body. Tony's equally determined to keep it till he's satisfied with the cause of death. If you two go round today, you can placate her. Explain the problem."

Brett grimaced but nodded. "We'll try."

"Good. Before that, check out the autopsy. After, make some inquiries. It'll just be the two of you for the moment. I can't justify a full-blooded team when I don't even know if there's a case here. Games had been ill for a few weeks, so it could be something natural, despite Tony's reservations. If we haven't got a cause of death, we have to explore a different angle. I want you two to find out if there's a motive for murder. If you come up with convincing evidence, I'll decide then if there are enough resources for a team." He stood up to bring the meeting to an end, or maybe he just needed to move again. He concluded, "You'll virtually be on home territory, Brett, because one obvious line of inquiry is the personnel at the drugs company. With your chemistry background, you'll know how their brains work. An ideal inquiry for you."

Brett and Clare got up to leave, saying in unison, "OK."

Before they slipped out of his office, Keith added, "And if you bump into any heating engineers, send them in."

It was compulsory to laugh at the boss's infrequent jokes, so they both grinned at him before closing the door.

Things were hotting up in reception. A young man was yelling his complaints at the Desk Sergeant as Brett and Clare passed through. "The university's accused me of pinching library books, but it wasn't me! I'm desperate! They'll chuck me off my course, you know."

"So you said," the Desk Sergeant replied. "But I'm not sure what you expect us to—"

Interrupting, the student wailed, "You think you've got better things to do with your time. It's just a few books, you say. But it's serious. It's my future. And they're not ordinary books. Someone's out to get me. Frame me for nicking them. You should be investigating who!"

The uniformed officer was acutely aware of the long queue. With as much patience as he could muster, he began, "Look, sir..."

Brett and Clare were about to leave him to deal with the situation when the lad pulled a penknife from his pocket. He flicked it open and waved the blade in front of the Desk Sergeant slowly and menacingly. He was like a cat about to pounce. The woman packing up the Christmas tree dropped a silver star and bolted for the door. Brett and Clare froze.

"You're not taking me seriously!" he bellowed. "But this," he said, bringing the knife closer to the officer's face, "has got your attention. Now, are you going to come to the library and check it out?"

Brett stepped into the fray. "Look," he said, showing his ID, "I don't think a knife's going to help your cause."

The student rounded on Brett. Glancing at his card, he exclaimed, "Lawless! Some name for a cop. At least I've got me a proper detective now."

"Yes, and I want you to give me the knife." He held out his hand. "Then I'll talk to you about your problem."

"No chance!" the young man snorted. He was intimidated by Brett's considerable frame. "You'll just bundle me away. Talk to me now. While *I'm* in control."

"No. I can't talk with a knife pointed at me. You'll have to hand it over first."

The student shook his head.

Clare joined her partner and said considerately, "I'm Clare Tilley. No silly name, but a cop all the same. What's *your* name?"

The young man eyed her suspiciously but replied, "Jordan Loveday."

A middle-aged man entered the station but seeing the tense confrontation, turned and immediately disappeared out of the door.

"OK," Clare said. "Now we're getting somewhere. The trouble is, Brett's right. We need you to put down the knife, Jordan. You could get into much more trouble over a knife than a few library books. Ordinary ones or not."

"But I didn't pinch them!"

Trying to calm the aggrieved student, Clare replied patiently, "I believe you. You don't look the type to go around nicking books. We should talk about it and see what we can do to help. You certainly don't want to risk your career over some library books. What's your subject anyway?"

"History," Jordan responded warily.

Clare smiled. "Not one of my strong points, I'm afraid. Anyway, we should go somewhere quiet and hear your side of the story, then take it up with the university."

"Really?" Jordan muttered, calmer now.

"Yes. I'll listen to you. I doubt if the university has. They've just made accusations, no doubt. That's the way of these things. People are quick to accuse, slow to listen." Gradually, she was asserting her authority and gaining Jordan's trust. "We need to find out what sort of books they were, why it's upset you so much and why the powers-that-be think you stole them. It's probably just a misunderstanding. But, to sort it out, you'll have to give me the knife. Then we can have a chat."

Two burly uniformed policemen strolled into the strangely silent room and, noticing that Clare was being threatened by a lad with a penknife, cried, "What's going on here?"

In that instant, Clare lost command of the situation. Straightaway, Jordan's growing confidence in her evaporated. He interpreted the officers' intervention as a trap, a diversion. He lunged at Brett.

Clare reacted like lightning. Before Brett could defend himself, his partner's foot appeared in front of him and slammed into Jordan's wrist. The knife was launched into the air like a lobbed tennis ball. Most of the occupants of the room ducked as it flew over their heads. Eventually, it clattered to the floor and skidded across the tiles until one of the policemen put a big boot on it.

Jordan clasped his right wrist and groaned. Looking up at Clare, he yelped, "You tricked me! And you've broken my hand."

As the two uniformed officers took hold of the student, she replied sympathetically, "No, I didn't trick you, Jordan. It was just bad luck, I'm afraid. I'd much rather talk than fight. I'm sorry about your wrist, but it won't be broken. Just sore. The doctor'll patch you up." She paused and then promised, "We'll still look into your problem."

As he was led away towards the cells, he hissed at Clare and Brett, "You're all the same! You don't care. You won't do anything about it."

Once the door had closed on the frantic student, the detectives sighed. Brett looked at his partner and said, "Thanks. You saved my skin there."

"Maybe," she replied dismissively.

Brett remembered that Clare was an expert at several styles of karate. While he had power and strength, she had reflexes and training. When there was any rough stuff, he could stand aside and let her deal with it – but he had to learn to renounce his natural chivalry.

"Well," Brett said to her, "we'd better get on with it. We'll have to come back later and provide statements on this little fracas."

Clare was still annoyed that her best efforts had been ruined by the chance entrance of two well-meaning policemen. And she had been stung by Jordan's closing accusation. "I suppose so," she muttered gloomily. "He'll be bailed on charges of threatening behaviour, carrying an offensive weapon, and who knows what else. All for some library books. It's crazy. Too crazy to let go. I think we ought to take an interest. Besides, I did say we would."

"Agreed," Brett replied. "We'll end up at the university sometime – I want to ask my old tutor if he knows anything about Colin Games – so we can check it out."

Clare nodded. "Good idea. He isn't really a thug,

our Jordan. It wasn't a fighter's knife. Too small. He wasn't even holding it in a way to do much damage. No real malice, just desperate – like he said."

As always, Brett was impressed by Clare. She had observed so much, so quickly. Her ability to judge character and situations in an instant reminded him that, despite his superior rank, he still had a lot to learn.

For once, the mortuary did not feel so cold. The universal chill lessened the effect of Tony Rudd's austere kingdom. Even so, few entered it without a shudder. Many averted their eyes. Tony was weighing the internal organs from a victim of a drugs overdose and spoke his findings directly on to tape. "Unequivocal. Fatal liver necrosis," he concluded. "Not a candidate for transplant," he remarked with dry humour. Thoughtfully, he pointed out the damage to his guests. Brett and Clare turned up their noses at the sight of the ravaged liver and waited for the distasteful ritual to come to an end.

To his assistant, Tony said, "Put the organs back in, sew up and hose down, will you? I'd better see to my visitors before they add to the mess. They're looking a bit green."

Scrubbing his hands clean, Tony muttered, "Paracetamol. Not a recommended way to go. Popular among suicides but I don't know why. Distinctly unpleasant. Several days of agony and then liver failure – unless truly massive amounts are taken to destroy the brain stem rapidly. Still, suicide's not your territory, is it? You've come to talk to me about Games. Yes?"

"Yes."

Tony Rudd dried his hands and said, "Good. It needs following up." He threw away the paper towels and, with relish, invited them to view Games's body.

"It's OK. A chat will do," Brett decided. "If you can't make anything of the body, I don't see how we'd help by looking at him."

"True," Tony rejoined. It was just through habit that he asked all of his visitors if they wanted to inspect a corpse. He enjoyed watching them squirm. Instead, he marched the young detectives to his office. "It's a fat file. The bullets, knives, blunt instruments and excess paracetamol are straightforward, brief reports. It's the mysteries that warrant a lot of words." He moved his long and steady finger over the touchpad of his laptop computer and then tapped it twice. "Colin Games. Forty-five-year-old chemist. Sturdy fellow, 178 centimetres tall. Bald as a billiard ball. Ill for the past five weeks, according to his doctor. No distinctive symptoms, just unwell. Fatigued. Not eating or drinking much. Low blood sugar – about fifty per cent of normal. Central nervous system disturbances – that's hyperexcitability and a couple of bouts of convulsions – but no obvious cause. Temperature was one to two degrees up, indicating a high metabolic rate. No infection detected. Now," Tony continued, "my findings. Died on the 3rd January. Hardly time to break his New Year resolutions. I can give you a list of disorders as long as you like but it doesn't add up to anything in particular. Body weight was far too low. Liver glycogen well adrift of normal. Evidence of defective cell structure. Anaemic. In fact, the red blood cell count, haemoglobin, serum glucose and cholesterol were all down. The kidneys were below par. Urine retention high. That means glomerular filtration rate and renal plasma flow were both low." He glanced from the screen to his two attentive but bewildered guests, saying, "I could go on for ever. Hyperplasia: enlarged liver and adrenal glands. Of course, the adrenals are essential for coping with body stresses so their impairment would increase the vulnerability to internal disruption, whatever it was. There wasn't a single live sperm anywhere, either. Sterile. As I said, lots of problems, but none of them on their own – except perhaps for anaemia – would be fatal."

Brett had not come across the Chief Pathologist very often but he'd noticed that Tony rarely personalized his subjects. After all, by the time that they came under his scrutiny, their personalities had departed. To Tony, they were merely collections of bones, organs and flesh to be dissected and analysed.

Brett asked, "Plenty of afflictions but no cause of death, then?"

Tony nodded. "You have an out-of-sorts victim. A partial loss of function almost everywhere that got to the point where life couldn't be sustained. At some critical level, terminal shutdown became inevitable. Like a big organization that struggles on for a while after losing the odd member of staff in different departments. To keep afloat, the other sections work harder, taking the strain. But when *they* have staff shortages as well, the whole system falls apart, going into terminal decline. What caused it? No one catastrophic factor. Just everything being below par. The summation of a large number of defects. That's what you've got here. I suspect that the renewal of blood-forming tissues, the reproductive organs and intestinal mucosa had all but ceased. I suppose the actual cause of death may have been the anaemia but it could have been dodgy renal function, hormonal imbalance, metabolic disturbance, faults in the central nervous system, cardiac irregularities or a combination of any of them. Take your pick. It still doesn't add up to a known disease."

"And it doesn't add up to a known poison?" Clare interjected.

"No. Not one that I've met before, and that's most of them." His face expressed frustration.

"But you suspect murder?" Brett enquired.

"All I know is that I have a chemist who's suffered an unexplained death. I can't prove foul play but *you* might be naturally suspicious. You might think the lack of a cause of death suggests a very clever method of killing. If you did, you might want to check out his colleagues in the pharmaceutical business. After all, they're experts at making substances that interact with the human body in cunning ways. Who knows what Games and his colleagues at PHP were working on?"

"Mmm. Tantalizing thought," Brett agreed. "We need to look for someone with a motive and who calculated that his death would be put down to natural causes – or a complete mystery."

"Over to you," Tony proclaimed.

The day had started cold and clear but, in the afternoon, a freezing fog gathered over the city of Sheffield. As daylight began to fade, the fog transformed Abbeydale Road into a string of orange smudges. All of the coloured Christmas illuminations in the windows along the road had been removed and the house lights that remained were obliterated by the murkiness. The beams of Clare's headlamps reflected off the droplets, producing a diffuse glow. The gritty slush on the road was threatening to revert to ice, so Clare drove gingerly. Approaching the smeared and dim red lights, she used the gears rather than the brakes to slow the car. Not confident of maintaining a grip on the slippery tarmac, she used the same technique to tackle bends.

"Did you ever see that film, *The Fog*?" she asked as she went down through the gears again.

"I don't think so," Brett replied.

"It's great stuff. Scary. A really creepy fog comes off the sea and engulfs this town. Then some dead pirates from a sunken ship come alive, invade the town and start wreaking revenge on the descendants of their enemies."

"Oh, yes," Brett said. "I know. I did see it. Sinister music. And the pirates used sharpened hooks and knives, if I remember rightly."

"I don't know about that," Clare admitted. "I had my eyes shut in those bits." Cautiously, she accelerated away from the traffic lights and headed for Dore, where Colin Games's widow lived.

Brett laughed. "You've just disarmed a real chap with a real knife and yet you can't look when it's all faked! They're just acting, you know. No one gets hurt."

Clare nodded and smiled weakly. She sidestepped the uncomfortable subject by joking, "Weird, isn't it? Still, we women are allowed to be contrary."

"Well, I'm glad you don't always close your eyes."

Deciding that Brett deserved an honest reply, she said, "I don't like knives. Never have, since I was little. It's worse when I can't do anything about it. When the threat's in front of me, I'm in command. That's all right. Watching it on the box is awful. I know what's going to happen and can't do anything to stop it, so I close my eyes."

"It still happens," Brett remarked, not realizing the extent of Clare's unease.

"Yes," she murmured sadly. She also knew, only too well, that it wasn't confined to films.

"I wish it was so simple with Colin Games. Someone with a grudge and a knife. Or a straightforward disease."

Outside the car, the roads were nearly deserted. Anyone with any sense had stayed at home. The fog was becoming more dense by the minute. On the left, the trees of Millhouses Park were bare skeletons. Beyond it, the railway and Hutcliffe Wood had vanished, dissolved by the gloom. If youngsters were sledging down the slopes of Abbey Lane golf course, they were hidden from view.

Clare turned right into Dore Road and cruised along it while Brett peered through the haze, looking for Stephanie Games's house. It turned out to be an old, large property, set back from the road at the end of a gravel drive. The tyres crunched on the loose stones as Clare rolled the car up to the house. As soon as Brett and Clare emerged into the biting night air and walked towards the front door, they were bathed in light from a movement detector. Stamping their cold feet on the doorstep and rubbing their hands, the police officers waited for an answer to their ringing of the bell. When the hall light came on and the door opened, a young man appeared. He was stout, about seventeen years old, and sported long black hair parted down the middle, slicked back and tied behind his head. "Yes?" he said, frowning.

"Detective Inspector Brett Lawless and Detective

Sergeant Clare Tilley," Brett announced. Both of them held out their IDs.

"Oh." The lad opened the door fully and stood to one side. "You'd better come in. Mum's in the shower. She'll be down soon."

He led the detectives into the lounge and awkwardly offered to take their coats. While he went to deposit them in the cloakroom, Brett and Clare remained on their feet and looked around. It was a long room, the lush curtains at the far end covering a patio door. In one corner, pine needles were adhering tenaciously to the thick pile of the carpet. The Christmas tree would have been installed before Colin Games died and removed cheerlessly afterwards. The furniture wasn't cheap. The grandfather clock was a genuine antique and the paintings on the walls were originals. The young man put his head round the door and said, "Take a seat. I'll go and tell her you're here."

Both Brett and Clare ignored the invitation and instead strolled round the room, glancing at the ornaments, papers, magazines, bookshelves and photographs. On the coffee table there was a mail-order catalogue featuring expensive female fashions. A striking gold-plated biro lay on the open page. Brett hesitated by a framed picture of Dr Games and his wife posing in the garden with a baby. They were sitting on a rug and squinting into the sun behind the camera. In the photograph, Colin Games was probably in his late twenties but he looked older because he was already going bald. Brett guessed that the child was the young man who had answered the door. He certainly featured in the next photograph. Smart in school uniform at the age of about twelve.

When the lad came back into the lounge, Brett pointed to the family photograph and said, "You must be Dr Games's son."

"That's right," he answered. "Dean."

"How old are you?" Brett enquired.

"Just turned eighteen."

Clare chipped in, "We're sorry about your father, Dean. But we have to ask some questions about him."

Brusquely, Dean muttered, "Do you know how he died yet?" Plainly, he was anxious and inquisitive. Not surprisingly, he also seemed emotionally disturbed by his father's death.

Softly, Clare responded, "No. Not yet. That's why we have to investigate."

Dean interrupted, saying, "Well, you've come to the—"

He fell silent as his mother, her hair still straggly and wet, strolled into the room. "Sorry to keep you waiting," she apologized. "Is it about Colin?"

Brett nodded. "Yes."

By unspoken agreement, they all sat down at the same time. Stephanie Games did so with a sigh.

Brett introduced himself and Clare and then explained, "We were just telling Dean that we don't yet have a cause of death, I'm afraid, so we have to ask you a few questions to build up a picture of him in the last few weeks."

"I've already spoken to someone."

"Yes," Clare interjected, "but do you mind if we go through it again? We've read the notes about your husband but there's nothing like getting it first-hand."

Stephanie shrugged. "All right." As an afterthought, she added, "Has Dean offered you a drink? He makes a super mug of coffee." She said it only because politeness demanded it. There was no enthusiasm in her voice.

Brett declined. "No, thanks."

Apparently, the shower had not refreshed Stephanie Games. She looked tired and glum. She did not seem to be completely devastated but then she'd had a few days to become accustomed to her bereavement. The worst shock was over. Probably, her husband's slow deterioration had also lessened the trauma of his death. She was in her early forties, rather plump, with short, dark hair. Her round face was not unattractive, more matronly than pretty.

"Can you tell us a bit more about your husband's illness?" Brett began. "We understand that he'd been ill for a while."

Stephanie took a deep breath. "Yes, you can say that again." She wiped away a drop of moisture from her cheek. It wasn't sweat or a tear but a trickle of water from her hair. "He didn't come out in boils or anything but he was decidedly under the weather. Tired, off his food. He was quite a big man but he lost an awful lot of weight. And … er … he wasn't easy to live with."

"In what way?" Brett queried.

"Oh, he'd fly off the handle at the smallest thing. His doctor called it overstimulation of the central nervous system. In other words, he was excitable, impatient. Tempers and convulsions. It wasn't easy, Inspector Lawless. You can love someone – someone who's obviously ill – and yet still find them almost unbearable."

Dean sat in silence and watched his mother with steely eyes. He did not dispute her appraisal of his father.

"After he'd had a real fling, he'd go quiet. Retire to bed and not eat or drink for ages. Those times, he was more pitiful than unbearable." She sighed before adding, "As I said, a difficult period."

"Did your husband's doctor put him on any medication?"

"Tranquillizers," Stephanie replied curtly. "They didn't do any good."

"Do you have any left? I'd better have them analysed to make sure they *are* what they're supposed to be – to rule out an error by the pharmacist."

"OK. Yes, there's still a bottle upstairs in the bathroom cabinet."

Without prompting, Dean rose and went upstairs, two at a time, to fetch the tablets. He was probably keen to grasp the chance to escape the scrutiny for a moment.

In the meantime, Clare asked, "I take it that your husband wasn't normally prone to such moods?"

"No," Stephanie answered. "All this started five or six weeks ago. Before that, he'd have the usual number of grumps. Nothing out of the ordinary. You know the sort of thing. The tiffs and squabbles every family has. He wasn't the most patient person in the world but he wasn't the least, either. That's right, isn't it, Dean?" she added, as her son clattered down the stairs.

Dean agreed. "Yeah. He used to be cool. No problem." He handed over the bottle containing a few pills.

"Thanks," Brett said thoughtfully. He was well acquainted with family discord. For as long as he could remember, friction had eroded his own relationship with his parents. He didn't know its source but its effect was obvious and destructive. He'd been rejected at an early age and it had hurt. Without brothers or sisters to turn to, he'd learnt to be independent. He grew up to be tough – and fragile. After leaving home, it was with relief that he went his way and his parents went theirs. As always, this Christmas he'd phoned them to wish them well. Courtesy and tradition required it. But he hadn't seen them for about eighteen months and they did not seem to be in a hurry to end the division. Brett was wondering how his mum and dad might respond if someone enquired after *him*. He guessed that they would smile and say, "He's doing well. A probationary inspector now, South Yorkshire Police force." Then they would change the subject before they had to admit that there was a rift. If there had been considerable discord in the Games household, it was possible that Stephanie and Dean would similarly deny it to outsiders. Brett could not decide if Stephanie was genuine. Her expression revealed little. He could be witnessing sincerity or a performance. He hoped that Clare, with her finely tuned intuition, was absorbing and assessing Stephanie's character.

"Colin worked at PHP," Brett said, shifting the direction of the interview. "Do you know what he was working on exactly?"

Stephanie smiled ruefully. "It's a secretive company. I should know. I work there as well. Still, I don't know *exactly* what he was working on. He was a synthetic chemist. Making new substances, that means. In the vitamins and hormones section. He was allowed to talk about most of it but not all – not even with me. A few months ago he prepared a new drug. That I do know. I suppose it would be a new vitamin or hormone. He was over the moon about it. Convinced it was going to be a big one. So big that he couldn't discuss it with *anyone*. The company was scared stiff that a competitor might get wind of it – or get hold of *him*. They upped his salary and started giving him all sorts of bonuses to make sure he wasn't tempted by offers from other drug companies. That's how we could afford to move here last year."

"What's his manager's name? I'd like to speak to him."

"Dr Raynor. Kelvin Raynor."

Brett turned to Dean and asked, "Your dad didn't talk to you about this drug, did he?"

Dean shook his head. "No. He knew I wouldn't be interested."

Addressing Stephanie again, Brett enquired, "Do you know for sure if he'd been approached by another drug company? And, if so, which one?"

"No, I don't know for sure but it's possible. Before he got sick, he said he'd met up with an old chemist friend at a meeting in London. Paul Dunnett. He works at Xenox now. Colin made it sound purely social but you never know."

"What's *your* line of work at PHP?" Clare put in.

"Totally different from Colin. I'm a biologist. I work in the animal house. We test the biological effects of potential new drugs on experimental animals."

"Have you had any problems with a test substance lately? Experimental animals becoming sterile and dying of anaemia, cardiac or kidney failure, metabolic imbalance? That sort of thing?" asked Brett.

Stephanie looked perplexed but answered the question anyway. "Not that I recall," she muttered.

"Do you get any bother from animal-rights groups?"

"Yes," Stephanie said. "The company's very touchy about it. They've already had an arson attack and two protests. Oh, and we had a threatening letter."

"Personally?" Brett asked. "It was sent here – to your house?" Seeing her nod, he continued, "Who – and what – did it threaten exactly?"

"We were never quite sure. It arrived a couple of months ago, addressed to Dr Games. Colin opened it, but it could've been for either of us. I suspect it was meant for the Dr Games who works with animals – me. But over the years I've found most people assume that the label of doctor applies only to men. If the extremists learnt that a Dr Games worked in the animal house at PHP, they'd probably think it was Colin. So, even if they meant to threaten me, they were probably gunning for Colin by mistake. Anyway, the letter wasn't specific about what they were going to do to us. Just give up the job or else."

"Have you still got a copy of it and the envelope?"

"No," Stephanie replied. "But you have. The police took it."

"And what did our colleagues recommend that you do?" Clare queried.

"A decent burglar alarm and security for the house. We were told to look under the car for suspicious packages before we used it. They also intercepted and checked out any parcels arriving in the post."

"Nothing else came of it?"

Stephanie shook her head.

"Interesting – and unpleasant," Brett murmured. He looked at her son and asked, "What about you, Dean? Still at school?"

The young man nodded. "A-levels at the college."

"Following in your parents' footsteps? Science subjects?"

Dean smiled wryly. "No. The opposite. Art, English literature and French." Behind the smile there was probably a real grievance. Perhaps he'd been hurt by a lack of support from his scientific parents.

"Do you have any idea when we'll get Colin's body?" Stephanie asked.

Brett replied regretfully, "I can't say, I'm afraid. We need to complete our inquiries. The Chief Pathologist is always reluctant to sign the release forms until he understands the cause of death. I know it's not very nice but I hope you understand."

Dejectedly, Stephanie nodded. "I suppose so."

"I've got an idea," Clare said across the top of the car outside the Games house, the chill making her breath visible. She looked as if she was speaking in smoke signals.

"Oh yes?" Brett replied suspiciously.

"I'm hungry. A meal and some good ale would go down well."

Brett grinned. "All right."

"There's a pub up the road in Totley. Excellent

fish menu." She ducked into the car before Brett could reply.

Sliding into the passenger's seat, he muttered, "You know how I feel about fish."

"You like them better swimming around than grilled," she baited him. "Only joking. There's a lot of other good stuff on the menu. You'll be OK." Pulling out of the drive, she added, "As long as you won't be too offended at the sight of me tackling a swordfish. Surely you don't think of swordfish as cuddly colourful creatures?"

"Well –" Brett hesitated theatrically and then said, "No, I'll allow you swordfish, I suppose."

The pub was warm with a real fire. Brett was soon seduced by the quiet and cosy atmosphere inside and its imaginative vegetarian dishes. Immediately, he realized that Clare was a regular because the landlord greeted her by name and asked if she wanted her usual pint of real ale.

"Just a half. I'm driving the boss so I've got to be careful."

The bartender smiled at Brett and asked, "The same for you?"

"Please. But I'll have a pint. I've got a lackey to drive me around tonight."

Clare snorted playfully. "We'll order some food as well, please. Mine's the swordfish steak. Not too heavy on the ginger. I want to taste the fish."

"And I'll go for your mushroom roast. My favourite," Brett commented.

"We aim to please the local constabulary," the landlord replied. "But usually sausages, chips, mushy peas and pies do the trick."

"You're not dealing with the riff-raff now, you know," Clare quipped. "The crack team has to look after itself." She tapped her stomach. Before she took her drink to a table, she asked, "No music tonight?"

"The folk group wouldn't brave the weather and the tape machine's bust."

"Pity," Clare uttered.

Brett breathed a sigh of relief. He preferred his pubs to be peaceful so that conversation was easy.

They stripped off their heavy coats and took seats opposite each other at a small table. Both of them held up their drinks and chirped, "Cheers." After taking a long draught, Brett said in a quiet voice, "What did you think of the female Dr Games, then?"

Clare put down her glass and thought for a moment. "Tricky," she pronounced. "Not as shaken up as I thought she'd be. A bit too composed and rational, perhaps. But not obviously a downright liar. Maybe you scientific types are always dispassionate about things. Still, I didn't disbelieve her but I couldn't quite trust her either. I'll tell you what, though," Clare continued. "I certainly want to speak to Dean Games on his own. Before his mother came in, he was going to say something to us."

"Yes," Brett agreed. "I got the impression it was going to be a spot of dissent. I'd like to know what."

"Yeah. He wasn't overwhelmed with grief for his

dad, either. I suspect it was a lukewarm family. You know – each of them getting on with their own lives, not paying too much attention to the other members of the household."

"Quite possibly," Brett murmured. Changing the subject, he said, "There's Kelvin Raynor – Colin Games's boss at PHP – and Paul Dunnett at Xenox to see, as well. I'm supposed to be in my element with people like them."

"Very funny," Clare responded with a smile. Seeing a puzzled look on her partner's face, she explained, "In your element with chemists? I don't remember much about chemistry at school but I *do* know it's all about elements."

Brett cringed. "Unintentional, I assure you. If I'd wanted to make a pun, I wouldn't have come up with such a *formula* joke."

Clare grimaced. After a brief bout of mocking laughter, she suggested, "Anyway, we need to chase up that threatening letter, as well."

"Yeah. I wonder if the documents section got anywhere with it."

"Well," Clare said, "what do you think? Do you reckon we've got a murder on our hands, or just a funny disease?"

"No idea," Brett admitted. "Impossible to say. We need a few more facts before we stand a chance of a decent theory."

"But you must be thinking about that drug he developed," Clare prompted.

"It's tempting," Brett replied, grinning mischievously. He could not resist the opportunity to speculate even though he was devoid of evidence. "PHP made it top secret because they thought it was going to be a huge profit-maker. But maybe Colin Games got contaminated with it – by accident or design – and, seeing the effect on him, PHP found out it's got drastic side-effects in humans. As a drug it's a dead duck, but they still haven't come clean about it. They haven't admitted that the new drug killed him. Why not? For one thing, they wouldn't admit liability because Stephanie Games would win a huge settlement from them if it was the company's fault. They'll try and cover up. Alternatively," Brett added, "some animal-rights group could have given him a dose of his own medicine. First a threatening letter and then they could've polluted him with what PHP was giving to its animals."

"Either sounds reasonable to me."

"Not quite, though," Brett declared. "You see, Stephanie worked in the animal house. Any new drug has to be tested on animals before it gets into humans. She's bound to know if a drug they were testing turned out to be a total disaster and killed their rats with symptoms similar to her husband's. She claimed she didn't."

"I see what you mean," Clare said. "She's a biologist. She'd have recognized Colin's symptoms as the same as those suffered earlier by some of her experimental animals."

Brett nodded. "The only problem with that idea is—"

"Ah!" Clare exclaimed, with pleasure. "My swordfish. Mmm. Smells good. Thanks."

Once the landlord had placed their meals in front of them and retreated, Clare asked, "So what's the problem?"

"Rats aren't human. That's the problem," Brett replied. "It's possible that the drug behaved itself perfectly well in experimental animals and was only toxic to humans."

"So," Clare surmised, "we can't rule out poisoning by a completely new drug made at PHP. That'd be why his symptoms are a mystery – never been seen before because it's a brand-new concoction."

"Of course, she could've been lying. As a biologist, she might have seen the effects of the drug on her rats and then decided to use it on her husband as well."

"Possibly," Clare replied. "But surely she'd know we'd check up on that."

"Yes. Tomorrow, we'd better pay PHP a visit. It should be an interesting day."

"And this," Clare added, pointing with her fork, "should be an interesting meal." She tucked into her swordfish with gusto.

Brett was an early riser. He liked to be out, taking his morning jog round the park before the road was awash with commuters. That way it was more peaceful, and he didn't have to fill his lungs with exhaust fumes. This morning, he ran more tentatively than usual. He did not feel entirely confident of his footing on the snow, ice and slush so he took it easy. In his wake, he left flimsy puffs of condensation. As he ran, he thought of the pharmaceutical industry in which he could have followed a career after obtaining his degree at university. There were several reasons why he chose a different direction. Working on drugs for the benefit of human health would have excited him but the business was driven by profit, not by benevolence. Brett was not convinced that he could put shareholders before customers. He was not sure that he relished making money out of people's ill-health. He was also put off by the animal experiments. He understood the need to test new drugs first on laboratory animals – he knew that the trials were a scientific necessity – but, even so, they made him feel uneasy. As he jogged past the dormant café, bemused ducks stood on the frozen boating lake and quacked plaintively.

By the time he returned home, he was hot on the inside and cold on the outside. After cleaning and warming himself in the shower, he gulped down a glass of chilled fruit juice. Then, taking his bowl of cereal and hot coffee into the lounge, he ate breakfast near his aquarium. Throughout the winter, as the temperature went up and down, his tropical fish swam in their own isolated and constant climate. The thermostat cushioned the discus fish, guppies and tetras from the whims of the weather. Brett kept them in an unnatural environment, just as PHP and Xenox kept their laboratory animals in cages. Both his pets and those animals were pampered and yet they were also imprisoned. Were the drug houses being any more cruel than Brett? He consoled himself with the thought that he did not subject his fish to untold indignities in the name of humanity.

It was evident, as soon as he walked into headquarters, that the heating system had been repaired. When he opened the door, he was hit by a blast of hot air. It was like walking into a furnace. The central heating had returned with a vengeance. Everyone inside had stripped to the minimum. Obviously, the engineer had set the temperature far too high. First, Brett despatched Colin Games's tablets to the Forensic Laboratory for analysis and then he plonked himself in front of his computer. Before driving to Pharmaceutical and Health Products, he rolled up his sleeves and scrolled through the chemical pathology results on Dr Games. Behind Brett, Clare read from the screen: "'Elevated amino acids, urea, creatinine, lactic acid and inorganic phosphate. Decreased levels of blood glucose and protein.' Do you understand all that?"

"I understand the words," Brett answered.

"But what does it *mean*? What does it tell you about Colin Games?"

"Not a lot. Actually, nothing. But there's something I learnt at university." He spun round to face Clare. "You can't know everything, so the next best thing to knowing an answer is knowing where to go to find an answer. I still want to visit the university and see Derek Jacob. Maybe we'll fit it in later or tomorrow. For now," he said, grabbing his overcoat eagerly, "it's a trip to Kelvin Raynor at PHP."

"Time to hit the arctic air again," Clare groaned.

The premises of PHP were surrounded by a sturdy high fence. The only way in was through the reception, which was actually a security office. One of the guards telephoned Kelvin Raynor to announce the arrival of the two police officers and to check that he would receive them. Once they had been granted an audience, they had to sign in and wear badges declaring them to be visitors to PHP. They were still not cleared to enter the site on their own. Another security guard escorted them into the appropriate building and delivered them to Dr Raynor's secretary. In her turn, she ushered them into a warm and plush meeting room where they were to wait.

In the corner of the suite, designed to entertain and impress visitors, there was a computer with a screen saver that threw garishly coloured balls continuously and hypnotically against the glass of the monitor. First, a tray of coffee and biscuits arrived, followed closely by Kelvin Raynor himself. He was a short, intense man with spectacles. He was dressed smartly in a suit and a tie that was as dazzling as the computer screen. Brett judged that he had given up working at the laboratory bench some time ago and now was a manager of his section. He worked with filing systems and accounts more than pharmaceuticals and apparatus. Clare gazed at Dr Raynor and detected a tense, cautious man behind the slick exterior.

"Good morning," he said as he took a seat opposite them. He placed his arms on the table, stared at them intently and enquired, "What can I do for you?"

Brett informed him that he and Clare were looking into the death of Colin Games and then remarked, "So, you can help us by telling us something about him. We gather he was one of your synthetic chemists. Was he happy here at PHP, what was he working on, had he upset anyone recently, had he had any particular successes – or failures – before his illness? Anything else we should know?"

Kelvin took a deep breath. "A tall order, Inspector Lawless. We'd better start with the coffee." Once he had pushed two cups towards his guests and taken one himself, he settled into his chair and began, "Colin worked with me for some years. I think I knew him pretty well. He was a splendid colleague. Certainly, I wouldn't say he'd made any enemies here. And I'm sure he was happy in his work with us."

Intervening, Brett asked, "Other companies hadn't tried to poach him, then?"

"They might have tried. I wouldn't know," he replied defensively. "But he wasn't unsettled, I assure you. We've got a good working environment here and we paid him well."

"So, he was a prized employee. Does that mean he *had* been successful recently?"

The manager took a sip of his coffee before responding shiftily, "He was working on new vitamins – and was doing a good job."

"What type of vitamins?" Brett queried. "Vitamins are a diverse set of chemicals that the body needs in its diet because it can't make them itself. And they have a variety of effects on humans. A drug company wouldn't set about making any old vitamin. You'd have a target."

Dr Raynor eyed Brett suspiciously. "You're right,

of course. He was preparing analogues of certain known vitamins." He seemed to hope that a dose of technical jargon would distract the police officers.

"That," Brett rejoined, "doesn't answer the question. I'm not trying to find out the chemical structures – you wouldn't tell me anyway to protect your products – but what biological activity was Colin Games aiming at?"

"I take it that you know something about pharmaceutical chemistry," Kelvin said, still evading Brett's enquiries. "Unusual for a detective."

"Perhaps," Brett retorted. "But I take it that Colin Games *did* make an important substance. Otherwise, you would have answered my question by now."

Kelvin hesitated and then reported, "Dr Games made several potential drugs that were based on vitamins. They're being tested for biological activity right now."

"But one must show particular promise," Brett inferred. "It must look good for curing some disease. What *is* its biological activity, Dr Raynor?"

"I'm not permitted to tell you that."

Brett sighed. He had had enough of the slippery chemist. "Who's got the authority to help us, then?"

"I don't understand what it's got to do with Colin's death."

"I would've thought that was obvious," Brett said. "Maybe it's got nothing at all to do with it, but we need to consider every option. What if this vitamin has certain side-effects in humans – like anaemia, hormonal imbalance, metabolic disturbance, convulsions? In short, what if it caused Dr Games's symptoms?"

"You're implying that he ingested the compound he made," Kelvin surmised. "Well, our laboratory procedures make the risk of accidental exposure negligible. Obviously, we can't stop someone who's determined to take substances of their own volition but our procedures forbid it and any sensible chemist – like Colin Games – wouldn't dream of doing it. If an employee did abuse the rules, we couldn't accept responsibility."

The manager's response brought a faint smile to Clare's face. He'd recited it as if he had rehearsed the speech before entering the room. As Brett had suggested last night in the pub, PHP was anxious to avoid liability and Dr Raynor was spouting company policy, not answering the question. "Are you aware that Colin Games took any of his own preparations?" Clare asked directly.

"Certainly not," Kelvin replied.

"And what about those symptoms?" Brett interjected. "Are they familiar? Do you have any compounds that caused something similar in animals, or anything in clinical trials that showed such side-effects?"

"No. If we had, it would be withdrawn immediately."

"OK," Brett said. "I come back to the activity of Colin's new drug. Who can tell us about it?"

"For that sort of information," Dr Raynor announced, "you'd need the Managing Director, Mr Schulten."

"Is he here? Can we have a word with him?"

"I believe that he'll be in tomorrow. We can check with his secretary if he can fit you in, but he's a busy man."

"This is an investigation into the death of one of his valued employees," Brett responded, in an attempt to apply pressure. "For such a serious matter, I'm sure he'd find us twenty minutes. Surely he owes Colin Games that much."

Before they left the site and handed in their visitors' badges, they secured a fifteen-minute interview for the next day with PHP's Managing Director.

Sitting next to each other at a small table, Brett and Clare peered at the envelope contained in a clear plastic sleeve. "Posted in Cumbria," Clare observed. "Anything else?"

Greta, the head of the Trace Analysis section, shrugged. "Not a lot. It was date-stamped a couple of days before Games received it. The name and address were written with a Pentel Ultra-Fine S570, according to a chemical analysis of the ink and the International Ink Library." She added, "In my section, we rely on the fact that, whenever two objects come into contact, some transfer of material from one to the other takes place. The trouble with the outside of this," she said, tapping the envelope while Brett still held it, "is that it's come into contact with too much. We can't tell anything from analysing the outside. The inside's a different matter, though. But the only significant trace evidence was a small fibre. We found a match with it in the database of fibres at the Home Office Forensic Science Service. It's from a dog, a retriever."

"What about the letter itself?" Brett prompted.

Greta extracted it from her file. Again it was protected inside a transparent wallet. She gave it to Clare who held it so that both she and Brett could read it.

You are responsible for torturing animals in the mistaken pursuit of more drugs. Animals have the same right to live without barbarity as human beings. You will stop your disgusting experiments on animals. If not, you will hear from us again. Human beings do not have a monopoly on the right to freedom and life. It may not always be the case that animals have a monopoly on being subjected to fatal experimentation.

Unsurprisingly, the letter did not bear a signature.

While Brett and Clare read it, Greta remarked, "Written by the same person with the same pen. The paper's from a standard W H Smith A5 writing pad."

"Any fingerprints?" Brett asked.

"Two partials but they're not good evidence. Even

if we found a match – which we didn't – they'd only tell us who'd handled the letter. Defence would claim that their client hadn't actually written it. The handwriting itself is a better fingerprint of the writer. If we got a match with someone's writing, defence wouldn't have a leg to stand on. We did ESDA analysis as well."

Halting her flow, Clare queried, "ESDA?"

"Electrostatic detection apparatus. When you write on a sheet in a pad, you make an impression of the words on the sheet underneath. It's usually tricky to see but ESDA's a way of visualizing it. Shows up really well. When we did it on this sheet," she said, tapping the letter, "we discovered that the same person had written a very similar message on the previous sheet. Sent to a similar vivisectionist, presumably. The graphologist suggested a right-handed woman wrote it, probably young, forceful and well educated."

"Mmm," Brett responded sceptically. He regarded psychological profiling by analysing handwriting as unreliable. With a wry smile, he quipped, "I suppose he could tell from the loopy letters that the writer's also an animal lover."

Greta understood his misgivings. "Graphology's not an exact science," she said, "but it's been helpful in some cases. In this one, we never did find out who wrote the letter but intelligence suggested the Campaign for Animal Rights was behind it."

"Intelligence?"

"Apparently, a few months ago, the rumour was that CAR was about to embark on something more than peaceful protests. As I understand it, half the companies who experiment on animals get a trusted employee to infiltrate CAR. That way, they get wind of any up-and-coming protests or positive action against their own labs. On top of that, one of the police forces had a man on the inside. A mole."

"Oh well," Brett joked, "if CAR discovers he's a mole at least they won't hurt him."

While they were in the Forensic Department, Brett and Clare called in at the chemical analysis section. There, they learned that Colin Games's pills were exactly what they were supposed to be – tranquillizers. Unfortunately, the solution to the strange cause of his death was not as simple as a mistake with his prescription.

Brett and Clare caught up with Paul Dunnett in the afternoon at his own house. The chemist from Xenox was off work with a heavy cold and his answers were interspersed with vulgar sniffs and violent sneezes.

After applying a dishevelled handkerchief to his red-raw nose, he snivelled, "Colin Games?" He acted surprised. "Yes, I knew him years ago – at university. York. He was pretty good, as I recall. I heard that he died. Sad, really."

"Haven't you seen him since your student days, then?" Clare probed.

Paul shook his head. "No," he stated, a little too emphatically and eagerly.

"Yet we heard that you'd bumped into him a few weeks ago," Clare continued.

"Who said that?"

"Colin Games said it – and then his wife told us," Clare replied bluntly. Then she gazed at Paul in silence, waiting for his discomfort to force him into a response.

"Well, actually, now you mention it, our paths did cross, quite by accident, at a chemical conference a couple of months back. For a minute, we talked about old times in the bar. It wasn't very memorable."

"It's hard to believe that it was *so* forgettable," Clare remarked. "If you put your mind to it, you'll probably be able to remember what you talked about."

"Er –" He coughed and then sneezed. "Excuse me. I hardly think our small talk would have much to do with his death."

"For example," Brett put in, "did he say what he was working on at PHP?"

Paul Dunnett grinned at Brett and, chuckling, asked, "Did you really say your name was Lawless? With a name like that are you sure you're cut out to be an upholder of the law? It's like the head of a nuclear-power plant being called Mr Greenpeace."

Brett tried, but failed, to force a smile at a witticism that he had heard a hundred times before. Besides, he suspected that Dr Dunnett was simply buying time to think. "*Do* you know what he was working on?" Brett repeated.

"I didn't ask," Paul answered in a gravelly voice that was filtered through catarrh. "We don't, generally. We all know in this business that the only thing people will talk about are old or failed drugs. None of us reveal our company's hot compounds."

Brett persisted because he believed that Paul Dunnett was being economical with his answers. Brett had not gained great insights into his character or his honesty but he'd noticed that the chemist had side-stepped the question. He also knew that there was an effective pharmaceutical grapevine. Whilst Xenox would not be aware of exactly what Colin Games had developed, there would be reasonably accurate rumours. "That's not what I asked," Brett said. "Do you know what Colin Games was working on? I imagine you had a good idea even *before* the conference."

Evasively, he muttered, "I think he was into synthesizing vitamins."

"Yes, but for what purpose?" Brett inquired.

Paul's nose did not need wiping, but he wiped it anyway and then coughed twice. More delaying tactics. He grimaced and then said, "Vitamins have a range of activities. I wish I'd taken more vitamin C for this cold. It could've been any one of a number of things, I guess."

"Like what? Are you saying he'd found a cold cure?"

"I wish he had. But not as far as I know."

"What then?"

"Why are you so keen to know?"

To show that he could be just as vague, Brett said, "Because his death and his work may be connected.

Now, do you want me to remind you that obstructing a police investigation is an offence?"

Paul Dunnett's illness had sapped his strength. He let out a sigh, sniffed and gave up the fight. "I heard he might have found a vitamin that promotes growth of hair."

Clare looked puzzled and glanced at Brett. The perplexed frown on Brett's face was rapidly disappearing. "I see," he muttered, almost to himself. "Interesting. That *would* be big news. The sort of substance a company like PHP would love to get its hands on, no doubt."

"Any pharmaceutical company would," Paul commented and then looked as if he wished that he had not made the remark.

"Why?" asked Clare. "What would it cure?"

Brett intercepted the question. "Baldness! How many more-or-less bald men do you know who are desperate enough to sweep their remaining strands over the top of their heads just to hide it, or buy wigs? They'd go crazy for a drug that promoted their own hair growth. A cure for baldness would be some money-spinner." He turned to Paul Dunnett and enquired, "You implied that Xenox would like to have this drug. Did you offer Colin Games anything to join Xenox, or to reveal the chemical structure of the drug?"

"It'd be foolish to pretend Xenox wouldn't take an interest."

"Meaning?"

Paul hesitated before he murmured, "Meaning Games wouldn't take the money."

"You mean, he refused to change camps – and he refused to reveal the drug's structure?"

"Not in so many words," Paul admitted. "He denied that he'd made a breakthrough. That means he really hadn't or the money didn't interest him."

"I see," Brett said. "Did you see him again after that conference?"

"No."

"Did anyone else from Xenox?"

Paul wheezed, "Not that I know of. I think he was out of our reach." He finished with an almighty sneeze.

As she drove back towards the centre of the city, Clare muttered, "I think there was more to that chat between Dunnett and Games. Dunnett was holding back. It could be that when he failed to persuade Games to give up his secrets or switch sides, Dunnett arranged a more permanent removal of the competition."

Brett agreed. "Possibly, yes. But once Colin Games had made the drug, killing him wouldn't stop its progress. The goose had already laid the golden egg." He exhaled loudly and then speculated, "Even if Colin Games didn't succumb to Xenox, PHP might have suspected that he did. They're all a bit neurotic about secrets in this game. Maybe he was seen chatting to Dunnett by some other PHP worker who went to the same conference. That *would* be a problem because PHP would do anything to stop its formula getting into the hands of another company. They might even have shut him up for good." He glanced at his partner and said, "Stephanie Games said the conference was in London. We need to follow it up. Get a list of everyone who attended, and who they work for. It'd be interesting if someone else from PHP was there."

Brett asked Clare to drop him at the university before she went on to the gym. Brett had an arrangement with the university's library. He could not borrow books but he had a pass so that he could use the reference section. He swiped his card at the entrance and went through the barrier. He wanted to know more about baldness and its causes.

After consulting several weighty textbooks in the biology section, Brett was surprised to discover that little was known about hair. Really, the factors causing hair to grow or to fall out were not properly understood. Stress, serious illness, exposure to radiation, malnutrition, hormonal imbalance or scalp disease could make humans shed their hair. Women's hair could fall victim to iron deficiency or pregnancy but the condition was rare and reversible. Brett found that by far the most common cause of baldness in men was ageing and it was genetic in origin. Baldness runs in families. Lurking behind hair loss were the male hormones, but the mechanism of their action was complex and unclear. He found that

ProGrow was the only licensed treatment for hair regrowth and many scientists claimed that it caused more false hopes than vibrant follicles. Some physiologists did not believe that it worked at all. Any hair that grew under treatment with ProGrow was fine like a baby's, and fell out again as soon as the expensive medication was stopped. After two or three years of treatment, balding seemed to begin again anyway. One author doubted the ethics of interfering with the normal ageing process in men for a condition that was not life-threatening. Brett took particular note of a reference to the possibility of synthetic analogues of vitamins A and D instructing DNA to reactivate hair growth. A vitamin could be a cure for baldness – at least in theory.

After an hour, Brett shut the last book and put it back on the shelf. Before he left, he went to see the Head Librarian. At the enquiry desk, Brett asked the assistant for Mr Huxford.

The Assistant Librarian was wearing a small badge bearing her name: Lynne Freestone. She was an old-fashioned prim woman in her fifties who looked like a retired teacher. Her eyes shifted around suspiciously and unpleasantly, apparently looking for troublemakers among the users of the library. "I'm sure *I* can help," she cackled.

"It's a personal matter," Brett replied. "I really need to speak to Mr Huxford."

Her eyebrows rose admonishingly. "If you insist," she muttered and went into a side room to call him.

When she emerged, she said, "Mr Huxford will be with you in a moment."

Lynne Freestone turned her beady eyes to another customer and Brett waited by the desk.

After a couple of minutes, the Head Librarian made his entrance. Seeing Brett lurking by the enquiry desk, he said, "Ah. Inspector Lawless." His memory for names and faces must have been phenomenal. He had seen the police officer only once before, when he had authorized Brett's pass to the library. "What can I do for you?"

"It's sort of business, I'm afraid," Brett began. "I hear that one of your students has been accused of stealing books."

"Books!" Mr Huxford exploded. "Books disappear all the time. At £20 to £100 a go, it's a drain on resources, but it's not disastrous. What's gone missing is much more than ordinary books. We're talking irreplaceable manuscripts and first editions, including Isaac Newton's *Principia Mathematica*. That's valued in the realms of £70,000. And a priceless manuscript from the eleventh century has gone as well." Plainly, he was outraged by the crime.

"What's the point of stealing them?" Brett asked. "Can they be sold on?"

"They'll turn up in an auction, no doubt. Or an antiquarian bookshop. It wouldn't be that tricky to sell them. They'd be presented as a family heirloom, no doubt. A great-great-grandfather's collection, or something."

"But they haven't turned up yet?"

"No."

"If they haven't been traced back to Jordan Loveday, what's the evidence against him?"

"Altogether, twenty items have disappeared. The computer tells me Loveday was working in the library shortly before each occasion when a manuscript was found to be missing."

"So, when someone comes into the library and uses a swipe card, the computer logs them in?"

"That's right," Mr Huxford confirmed.

"Mmm. Not really conclusive, is it? Was anyone else in the library each time?"

"No."

"Could anyone get into the library without using a pass, so the computer wouldn't register them?" Brett asked. "What about the library staff?"

Mr Huxford looked shocked and offended. "We *all* have passes. Students *and* staff."

"Someone must unlock the library, get in and turn the system on. That person's in without using a pass."

"That person is me, Inspector Lawless. And you can't seriously accuse the Head Librarian –"

"No," Brett responded. "Of course not." It was too early to accuse *anyone* but Brett would not discount Huxford just because he had risen to the lofty position of Head Librarian. Brett thanked Mr Huxford and made his way to the exit. To leave, he had to use his pass again so that the computer recorded his departure. As soon as he pushed through the waist-high barrier, he stopped and turned. Waiting until the staff at the issuing desk were not looking, Brett placed his big hands on the top of the barrier and vaulted over it in a single energetic leap. He was convinced that anyone who was reasonably athletic, and who wished to bypass the computer, would be able to get over it without using a card.

Brett returned to Mr Huxford and said, "Something else I meant to ask. Can you consult the computer at any time and get a list of who's in the library?"

"Yes," he replied. Seeing in Brett's eyes an invitation to try it right now, he tapped the keyboard and, after a moment, said, "I have it in front of me. Alphabetical."

"And what about me – under Lawless? Am I here?"

Mr Huxford's eyebrows rose. He glanced up at Brett and murmured, "No. You're not. You left two minutes ago."

"Mmm. Makes you think, doesn't it?" Brett strode back to the barrier and, knowing that Mr Huxford would still be watching him, vaulted over the security barrier again. From the other side, he turned and smiled meaningfully at the Head Librarian.

At the age of thirteen, Clare had watched aghast as her father was attacked by a thug wielding a knife.

Her dad had not been fatally injured but he was seriously hurt. It wasn't his wounds that so dismayed the young Clare but her own utter helplessness. She'd been petrified, unable to react. She'd experienced a stomach-churning coldness as if she had been plunged suddenly into icy water. She never wanted to feel that way again. She hadn't vowed on the spot to become a police officer and a martial-arts expert, yet she believed that the incident had played a part in fashioning her life. As soon as she was sixteen, she left school and joined the police force.

Now, she lived alone. She'd had a number of boyfriends but none had stayed the course. Her role as a police officer always seemed to dictate her life – including her social life. She was content with the situation, though. She was fulfilled more by her job than by a boyfriend. It was just that sometimes, during a long, cold evening on her own, she wished that there was someone else around.

She took a book from her heavily laden shelf but, before she indulged herself with poems and a pint of real ale in front of the open fire, she thought of Jordan Loveday. "The book snatcher," she commented wryly to herself. She put her own book on the armchair and went to phone Brett, asking if he'd made any progress at the library.

Brett updated her and concluded, "Anyone reasonably agile could've got in without triggering the computer and pinched the books. It could be just bad luck that Jordan was in the library each time. An amazing set of coincidences, but there's no real evidence against him. It was good enough for the university's disciplinary committee, it seems, but there's nothing you'd want to put before a jury."

"Did you tell the librarian what you thought?"

"Sort of. I gave him a practical demonstration that'll sow a few seeds of doubt."

"Well done." Clare hesitated before adding, "Are you on your own at the moment?"

"Yes. Just relaxing."

"I don't suppose you want –" Clare stopped and sighed. "Oh, nothing. Forget it. It's a rotten night for travelling. I'm going to curl up on the sofa with a good book then get to bed early for a change."

"Sounds nice," Brett replied. "See you in the morning."

Mr Schulten was a big, imposing man. Seated behind a large antique desk at PHP, he looked at his two visitors severely, as if expecting a confrontation. Even so, he answered questions concisely, politely and precisely. "Colin Games," he pronounced. "Vitamins and hormones. A good man. I was very sorry to hear of his death. A loss to the company, and to his family. I know Stephanie and Dean, and I know they'll miss him very much."

"We know he was working on the synthesis of new vitamins," Brett said, "but it would help our inquiries to know the goal of his research. Dr Raynor suggested that we speak to you."

"Why would that information help?"

"We want to rule out a connection between his work and his death."

"I have to be very protective of my business interests," Mr Schulten replied.

"Would it help if I said we've already heard that Dr Games had come up with a treatment for baldness?"

Behind his desk, Mr Schulten stiffened. "Who told you that?"

"Someone at Xenox," Brett confessed. "You'll be pleased to hear he didn't know any details."

"Xenox," Mr Schulten mumbled spitefully. "Well, I can confirm that your contact's right but I trust that this information will be confined to ourselves. I'm sure that, as police officers, you're aware of the need for confidentiality."

"Of course," Brett assured him.

"You may well realize the enormous value of a cure for baldness. To date," he stated, "there's no known cure. There's only ProGrow, which is barely a short-term solution and certainly not a long-term one. Yet worldwide it grosses over £200,000,000 per year. Just think of the commercial potential of a real cure for baldness." Mr Schulten paused and, to lighten the conversation, added, "You may be aware of various quack treatments. The Office of Fair Trading is clamping down on the most outlandish claims. A book proposing rubbing cow pats on to the scalp and standing upside down has just been banned from claiming it promotes hair growth. The authorities have given dubious authors – and more respectable manufacturers – every opportunity to provide data that show their nonprescription products really work. None did. Our drug prepared by Colin Games appears genuinely to stimulate hair growth in cases of male pattern baldness – that's genetic hair loss."

Exasperated, Clare put in, "Forgive me, Mr Schulten, but I thought a pharmaceutical company like yours was supposed to be improving the lot of humankind by finding cures for diseases. Pampering the vanity of men – bald men – seems too trivial for all the effort you're putting in."

Mr Schulten laughed, but not unpleasantly. "We are not a charity, Sergeant Tilley. Our shareholders require profitability. Pharmaceutical products must be commercially viable as well as desirable and safe. A cure for baldness is likely to be the biggest-selling medication of all time."

"You keep referring to a cure," Clare objected, "but there isn't a medical problem here."

"I have to disagree. Male pattern baldness *does* constitute a medical condition. It adversely affects the quality of life of many men, especially when it occurs prematurely in young men who don't wish to be at odds with their contemporaries. You shouldn't underestimate the misery and psychological problems it can cause. As such, it deserves and requires intervention."

"I thought being bald was all the rage," Clare countered.

"If some wish to sport a bald head as a fashion accessory, that's fine," Mr Schulten declared. "But men shouldn't have to suffer the indignity of *unwanted* hair loss. For those men, in the future, we'll be able to alleviate the suffering."

Clare was still offended by the company's policy. "It strikes me," she objected, "that there are such things as profitable but trivial problems like baldness and colds, where cures are very lucrative. But what about the really horrible diseases like Parkinson's or the mad cow problem, whatever it's called? Shouldn't you be working on those, or aren't they profitable enough?"

Trying not to sound patronizing, Mr Schulten replied, "If our new cure for baldness makes it on to the market, it'll earn PHP huge sums of money. That's not something I'm ashamed of. In fact, it's excellent. Success in this sector is very fragile. It relies on just a few highly profitable best-sellers. Much of that profit will be used to fund research into the serious but less commercially viable sectors. That includes Parkinson's and Creutzfeld-Jakob disease. I repeat, Sergeant Tilley, this company isn't a health charity. It's a business."

"As interesting as it is to discuss the ethics of the pharmaceutical trade," Brett interjected, "we need to progress our inquiries. Thanks for clarifying Dr Games's work and obviously we'll bear in mind the sensitivity of the information you've given us. One final question. Did Colin Games try his own preparation on himself? I couldn't help noticing that he was bald."

"Unlikely," Mr Schulten answered swiftly. With a smile on his face, he explained, "Colin's drug works. If he'd taken it, he would have died with a full head of hair."

The afternoon sun was no match for the thick band of cloud that hovered over Sheffield. The day remained dull and cool. The road was clear of ice and snow but the pavements and parks were dirty-white and slushy. As Brett and Clare neared the sixth-form college, Brett glanced across the road at the field. "Hang on, Clare," he said urgently. "Pull over a second."

Clare stopped the car by the kerb, and leaving the engine running, asked, "What is it?"

"Look." Brett pointed to a couple wrapped in heavy coats, taking a lunchtime stroll in the grounds opposite. It was Dean Games, ambling towards the college, hand-in-hand with a young woman. In her other hand, the girl held a lead. At the end of the taut lead, a dog pulled this way and that, picking up scents in the squelchy paste underfoot. "A young woman with a retriever," he murmured, thinking about the psychological profile of the writer of the threatening letter and the dog hair in the envelope.

On the same wavelength, Clare added, "I wonder if she's right-handed, well educated and forceful."

Coming through the thin line of sad trees to the roadside, the couple stopped and exchanged a few words, enveloping each other's heads briefly in a fine cloud of condensation, and then kissed. Dean crossed the street and the young woman headed back across the park.

"Shall I follow the girl," Clare asked, "while you tackle Dean?"

"No. We'll keep to the plan," Brett decided. "We'll both collar Dean. We're more likely to find out about his girlfriend by asking him than we are by tailing her."

"Fair enough," Clare replied, accepting his judgement without question. Glancing over her shoulder, she pulled away from the kerb and turned into the college car park.

Just inside the building, there was a filthy pool of water, left by myriad boots and shoes. It was a mixture of melted snow and mud. Brett located Dean almost immediately. Still huddled in his coat, he was talking to a friend in the reception area, made cold by the frequent opening of the doors. When Dean saw the two detectives, he said goodbye to his fellow student and faced them. "Hello," he muttered cheerlessly. "Are you after me?"

"Just a few questions," Brett replied. "Is there anywhere we can go?"

Frowning, Dean thought about it. "Classes are about to start. The common room'll be more or less empty and I've got a study period, so we can go there." Still looking suspiciously at them, he invited them to follow him.

They sat in a corner of the common room with its four garish walls covered with a mural that had been painted by the students. Dean's own contribution to the painting was a scantily clothed and muscular female fantasy figure with a colossal shining sword. "It's … striking," Brett complimented him. "Very good."

"Yes, but you haven't come to give me marks for art."

"No," Brett admitted. "There's a couple of things we'd like to ask you. Like, whether your dad was bothered about being bald. Did it depress him?"

Dean was taken aback by the unexpected question. He shrugged. "I don't know. I don't think so. He'd had plenty of time to get used to it." His face creased as he thought about it. "I think Mum said he was sensitive about it when he was younger. But I didn't see any sign of him worrying about it."

"Do you have a girlfriend, Dean?"

"You do ask some funny questions. What's it got to do with you?"

"Just trying to paint a picture of everyone in the Games household."

"I've never taken her home but, yes, I have."

"We couldn't help seeing you with a young woman outside. Was that her?"

Dean nodded unwillingly.

"What's her name?" Clare enquired.

He hesitated before answering, "Hannah Farr."

"What does she do?"

"She's at the university up the road. First-year history student."

Clare glanced significantly at Brett before enquiring, "Is she a native of Sheffield?"

"No. She comes from Whitehaven," Dean snapped.

"Whitehaven in Cumbria?" Brett asked.

"Yes." Plainly, Dean was losing patience. "Look. I don't know why you're asking about Hannah. You should be checking –" He ground to a halt.

"What?" Brett asked sharply. "You did the same thing when we saw you at home. You were about to say something dramatic but your mother came in and interrupted you. She won't here."

"Yeah. Well. It's her you ought to be checking out," he said quietly but positively.

"Your mother?"

"Aren't most murders domestic affairs?"

"Murder?" Brett queried. "We're only investigating a death. Have you got any reason to suspect murder?"

Dean seemed to be restless and highly strung. "You wouldn't be going to all this bother if you thought it was natural."

"We haven't come to any firm conclusion yet," Brett remarked. "Now, why do you want us to check out your mum?"

Dean braced himself and said accusingly, "She's done pretty well out of it. Half his estate in his will. And now she doesn't have to fetch and carry for Dad. You see, Dad didn't believe in sharing the chores. He always expected Mum to do the housework, make the meals and shop – even though she worked at

PHP as hard as he did. On top of that, she's free to carry on with a guy called Michael Ashton."

"Michael Ashton?"

"She thinks I don't know she's got a lover."

"So, you'd describe your parents' relationship as not entirely harmonious?"

"No punches thrown. Nothing much said. Just preoccupied with their own lives. No love, as far as I could see. I reckon they stayed together out of habit. That's all. We were a … loosely hinged family."

"This hunch about your mum. Do you have any real evidence against her? Do you have any hard evidence that your dad was murdered?"

"No and no," Dean answered tersely. "That's your job, not mine."

"Where does Michael Ashton come from? Is he from round here?"

"I think so. You'll have heard him. One of the presenters of the local-radio morning programme. You know. News, traffic reports, silly quizzes and telephone debates. That sort of thing. Basically," Dean said with venom, "he's an opinionated know-all. Mum met him when she went into the studio to do an interview on animal experiments. After that, she called him from the house a few times. I overheard once or twice."

"I understand your difficulty, Dean," Clare said softly. Perceptively, she added, "Are you worried about living at home with your mum?"

"Why do you think I'm telling you all this?" he

growled. "Of course I'm worried. If she's done Dad in for half his money, she'll be after the other half soon. Dad left it to me."

Clare nodded slowly. She said, "Don't forget that we haven't even established how he died, never mind who might have been responsible for it. If anyone."

"That's what bothers me. Your lack of progress," Dean retorted. "I've not been feeling so good recently. Nothing too serious, just more tired than usual. What if she's started doing to me what she did to Dad? I wish you *were* on to something," he said with agitation in his voice. "It might give me some hope that you'll come and rescue me."

"Don't worry," Clare concluded reassuringly. "We'll be keeping an eye on the situation. Have you been to see your doctor?"

"No."

"You should," she suggested. "And be sure to tell us if you get any worse."

As a parting shot, Dean muttered, "How bad do I have to be before you'll believe she murdered Dad?"

Back at headquarters, Clare's request for information from the Association of British Pharmaceutical Companies had been answered by fax. The message was simply a list of people who had attended the Association's annual conference last November, together with their affiliations. Glancing down the register, Clare spotted the name of Dr Kelvin Raynor.

"We've got ourselves a suspect and a motive," she announced. "Raynor could have seen Colin Games talking to Paul Dunnett in London. He denied it when we spoke to him but he would, wouldn't he?"

"Yeah," Brett replied. "We've got ourselves a whole load of suspects and motives. Time for a list." Ironically, he added, "Plenty of suspects but we may not have a murder."

The investigation had not been accorded an incident room with whiteboards and flip-charts so Brett used a pad of A4 paper instead. He talked it through with Clare, writing notes as they discussed each possibility. He followed each name with a possible motive and the likelihood that they knew enough about chemistry to concoct and administer a devious and elusive poison.

Dr Kelvin Raynor.	*Protecting drug discovery on behalf of PHP after seeing Games talking to Xenox representative (Dunnett). Has plenty of chemical and biochemical knowledge.*
Mr Schulten (PHP).	*Same as Kelvin Raynor. May not have sufficient scientific knowledge.*
Dr Stephanie Games.	*Unfaithful wife and beneficiary. Has necessary chemical and biochemical knowledge.*
Michael Ashton.	*Probably Stephanie's lover. Removal of rival. Knowledge of chemistry unknown.*
Hannah Farr.	*Animal-rights protestor? No known scientific knowledge.*
Paul Dunnett (Xenox).	*No obvious motive but connected with drug. Had*

Games promised information to Xenox in return for cash, but not delivered? Had Games given him incorrect information to throw him off the scent? If so, revenge or anger is the motive. Plenty of chemical knowledge.

Note: *Was Games playing both companies off against each other for more cash? If so, either might want him out of the way as too demanding.*

Dean Games. *No known motive or scientific knowledge. Alleged sickness could be a front, to divert suspicion. Maybe he's the one after the family fortune, not his mum, as he claims.*

Once they had exhausted their ideas on suspects, Brett wrote underneath the list, "But is it murder? What killed Colin Games?"

"You know," Clare said to Brett, "the problem entries are Hannah Farr and Michael Ashton. We don't know enough about them yet."

"Exactly," Brett agreed. "They're our next targets." He planned to assemble as much information as he could on the suspects and then to start eliminating them. He was also desperate for information on the cause of death. A trip to the university would allow him to check out Dean's girlfriend and to get the opinion of his old tutor, Professor Derek Jacob. Yet, when he looked at his watch, he realized that it was too late to catch Hannah Farr on campus. "Let's get an address for Michael Ashton and pay him a visit tonight," he suggested. "We'll do the university, my tutor and Hannah Farr tomorrow."

"OK," Clare agreed. "We could drop in at the library in the morning as well, to see if anything's happened about the Jordan Loveday business since your visit last night."

They knocked, then waited outside Michael Ashton's house for a long time before he responded. In the doorway he squinted at the detectives' ID and groaned. "You'd better come in," he grunted. "Hopefully not for long. I was just getting ready for bed." As Clare walked past him, his eyes followed her lustily.

Entering the short hallway, Brett glanced at his watch. Eight o'clock.

Michael Ashton muttered, "It might be early for you but it's midnight by my internal clock. I have to be up for work at four." Assuming that everyone in Sheffield knew who he was, he added, "A moment's thought would've told you that."

"Oh yes," Brett replied. "The morning programme. Well," he said as he was shown into the living room, "we'll try and make it quick."

Flopping into an armchair, the broadcaster murmured, "What's it all about anyway?"

"Let me ask you bluntly, since you want to get this interview over with – what's your relationship with Stephanie Games?"

"What's it got to do with you?" Ashton rejoined.

"We're looking into her husband's death," Brett replied, not concealing anything. Following his familiar line, he said, "To do so, we need to build up a picture of the Games family. Your name cropped up as being part of that picture."

"Mmm." Ashton's expression suggested regret. "Yes, I know Stephanie. I think it was six months ago we met. She came on air to defend the case for sacrificing experimental animals in the name of medical advances. She was a good performer."

Clare watched Michael Ashton critically. She was not sure that the killing of animals was justified if the big medical advance was a cure for going bald. She tried to remember that her job was to judge Ashton, not the pharmaceutical industry. With growing annoyance, she noticed that he kept staring at her hungrily. His lecherous eyes had surveyed every millimetre of her body. His unwanted attention made her shudder. Michael Ashton was supremely confident and composed, even though he was clearly tired. Dean's assessment of him was probably accurate. Clare anticipated that, if Ashton were involved in murder, he would not let it slip. The evidence against him would have to be undeniable before he would crack.

"We … er … hit it off. At first. But—"

Interrupting him, Brett asked, "By that, you mean you had an affair?"

"Yes, but it didn't last long. Or at least it shouldn't have. I'm a popular person," he boasted. "When I'm not in the studio, I'm doing guest appearances and charity work. I meet a lot of people. A lot of women. I wanted to end it with Stephanie pretty quickly but she wouldn't let go. Kept calling me. She'd drop in after work." He sighed. "Tiresome. She wouldn't take a hint."

Clare leant forward and said, "When did you last see her, Mr Ashton?"

"I can't remember."

Immediately, Clare detected a lie. "Was it weeks or days ago?"

His response was intentionally vague. "Not very long ago."

"And what would you say if I told you we have a reliable witness who saw the two of you together in the past week?"

He shrugged his big frame. "They're probably right."

Of course, Clare had no such witness, but Ashton fell for it. "So, you're not trying *that* hard to shake her off."

"She's a persistent woman, my dear."

"Sergeant Tilley's my name," Clare snapped at

him. "And I'm sure a man of the world like you would be able to give a woman the cold shoulder if you really had a mind to," she added.

Michael Ashton sank back into his chair and stretched his arms like a peacock showing off its plumage. "Let me put it this way," he boomed. "If all else fails, Stephanie's available."

"I see," Brett said, trying to hide his distaste. "Did you ever meet Stephanie's husband?"

"I tend to shy away from husbands."

"So you didn't?" Brett checked.

"No."

"And since he died, have you seen more of Stephanie Games? Have you taken advantage of his absence?"

"I wish he was still with us," Ashton barked. "Then she wouldn't have so much opportunity to pester me."

"So you *have* seen more of her?"

"No. But I've had to be elusive not to see her more."

"OK," Brett said. "I get the general picture. One last question. Before you were a radio presenter, what did you do?"

"Just about everything. I've been a journalist. Tried my hand as a writer. I've even worked on a farm and had a spell in local government. Seen quite a bit of the world."

"Have you ever worked in science?" asked Brett.

"No, but it fascinates me. Maybe I'll do that next.

I'm not one of those people who believe there are some things that they just can't do. If I put my mind to it –" He stopped himself, saying, "I'm slipping into radio talk when I should be slipping into bed."

Brett and Clare stood up. "All right. We'll leave you now. If we need to see you again, we'll try and catch you earlier in the day."

"Oh, I'm sure my image on your tapestry of the Games family is as complete as it needs to be. As you know, I'm not in the foreground, just a shadow in the background. And I certainly had no desire to be rid of Colin Games."

Brett gazed at his tropical fish. Some flashed energetically from one end of the aquarium to the other as if they were competing in races. Others, mostly the larger occupants, drifted casually or idled on the spot like spectres. He enjoyed watching them. They soothed him, helped to cast off the badness that a police officer inevitably meets and must shed. He wondered, though, if it was possible to feel true affection for his untouchable, colourful companions. He doubted it because mere fish could not give anything back. Since Zoe's death, he hadn't sought another outlet for his affections. Like the fish, she was untouchable. A mere memory. Unable to give anything back.

His mind drifted to the death of Colin Games. Whichever way he turned in the investigation, he came across animals. The threatening letter. The experimental animals at PHP. Even Ashton had worked on a farm. If Games had been murdered, perhaps it was something to do with animals. Perhaps he had been used in an experiment that had gone very wrong? Maybe Colin Games had been a human guinea pig. It was an unpleasant thought but, in the absence of more facts, it was just as likely as any other theory. Instead of sleeping, Brett stared at the ghostly glow of his aquarium and replayed the dead man's obscure symptoms.

During the night, a vicious wind from Siberia blew right across the continent, dispersing the clouds over Britain and turning the partly thawed snow to glass. The temperature plummeted. Several degrees of frost laid siege to the city of Sheffield. Roads became ice-rinks, cars left outside were sealed inside a thick layer of transparent ice, their doors refusing to budge, and people on the streets became unstable bundles of clothing that belched clouds of breath like struggling steam trains. The day was punctuated with flurries of dry, powdery snow, which the wind pushed until it lodged against kerbs, walls and banks. Any stationary object suddenly acquired white contours.

Brett and Clare breached the chalky outline of the Department of Chemistry at the university. Clare felt a degree of trepidation. She had never been in a university and her experience of chemistry was restricted to the images in films. Mad scientists doing unspeakable things with horrible poisons or lethal explosives. In reality, Professor Derek Jacob was a pleasant, sane, dedicated man who was eager to explain his work to her. He was certainly not the type who laboured late into the night behind closed doors, plotting the downfall of the human race. Quite the opposite. He was researching the cause of some rare but life-threatening diseases. At one point, he turned to his former student and commented, "I know it isn't politically correct to say so any more, Brett, but now I've met your partner, I understand why you're working in the police force!"

Clare smiled, knowing that the chemist was not patronizing her but conferring an innocent compliment. Michael Ashton had leered at her as a mere object but Derek was appreciating her curiosity and demeanour, not just her good looks.

"Having a partner in the force means something different from having a partner in normal life," Brett replied with a grin. Switching the conversation to business, Brett continued, "Really, I came to ask you about a death. One that's puzzling us. A forty-odd-year-old chap." He reeled off the symptoms like a memorized list of football results. "Fatigue. He was off food and drink. Elevated amino acids, urea, lactic acid and phosphate. Low levels of blood glucose, cholesterol and protein. Bouts of convulsions. High temperature. Dodgy cell structure. Anaemia. He had an enlarged liver and adrenal glands and he was sterile." Brett continued the roll call of symptoms until he concluded, "Obviously, he was suffering metabolic disturbance."

Derek's eyebrows rose. "Is that all?" he queried impishly.

"I doubt it," Brett replied. "I probably forgot a few."

"Phew! That's quite a catalogue for one human being. Sounds more like the symptoms of a whole ward of patients."

"No. It's all one man," Brett assured him. "Have you ever come across anything like it? In your time, you must have seen some funny metabolic diseases."

"Sure. But nothing like that. All my diseases, I can pin down to something specific. Inability to get energy from fats, amino-acid metabolism in disarray. Your man seems to have suffered from everything. Tell you what, though," Professor Jacob added, "I'm curious. I'll agree to do what you really came here for."

"Thanks. How about if I bring some of his urine to you tomorrow?"

"Fine. Your pathologist should have kept a sample from his bladder. Try and get him to give you a couple of normal samples for comparison. Best to have them from dead males of the same age who haven't gone down with disease. A couple of road-accident victims would do it." Seeing Clare frown, perplexed by their exchange, Derek explained, "We all have organic acids in our urine. Hundreds of them. If your victim had some weird metabolic disorder, his organic acids would be different from the normal ones. I've got the equipment to analyse urine for them. That's what we're talking about. Tomorrow morning," he added, "you remind your partner that last time I did him a favour for nothing, he promised to find a budget to pay me next time."

"Must have caught him in a hopelessly optimistic mood," Clare put in happily.

As Derek escorted them to the door, Brett said, "You do a bit of business with PHP, don't you?"

"They put a few morsels my way sometimes," the chemist replied.

"Any rumours about them, at all?" Brett enquired. "Unsettled staff, internal quibbling, that sort of thing."

"Do acids react with bases? Of course. It's a hotbed of intrigue. Like all industries these days. When jobs are in short supply, everyone's looking after themselves. Knives out for colleagues. Outsiders don't see the hostility and back-stabbing but it's there. Like molecules – never seen but always there."

"Anything specific? I'd be particularly interested in rumours about Colin Games."

"I knew him by name but I didn't really know him as a person. I'm not enough of an insider. The company seemed to think a lot of him, though. That means he made a few worthwhile compounds. He was bright or lucky, I guess. I've got a colleague who knew him a long time ago. Roger Bassindale at York. When Colin Games was a student there, Roger was his supervisor. Anyway, at PHP, I suggest you assume that all those employees who seem to be the best of friends are actually in fierce competition, trying to avoid redundancy, exploiting each other's weak points." He opened the door for them and asked, "Do I gather that it's Colin Games's urine we'll be looking at tomorrow?"

Brett put his forefinger to his lips. "I couldn't possibly comment."

Derek beamed. "I'll take that as a yes." Then, seriously, he added, "Pity. We all become a urine sample in a chemical pathology lab eventually."

In the Humanities Faculty, the departmental secretary soon confirmed that Hannah Farr was a student in the first year of a history degree. Then she directed Clare and Brett to Hannah's personal tutor, Dr Ian Matanda. Luckily, Dr Matanda was in his office so Brett was able to request a sample of Hannah's handwritten work.

Wary and protective of his student, the tutor enquired, "Is Hannah the subject of an investigation?"

"No, not as such," Brett responded. "We need a sample of her handwriting hopefully to rule her out of an investigation."

Dr Matanda sighed. "OK," he muttered unwillingly. From a filing cabinet, he plucked out her last essay and showed the front page to Brett. "Shall I photocopy the first couple of pages for you?"

"Yes. Thanks. That'll be fine. Especially if you can copy them on to clear acetate sheets."

Three minutes later, Ian Matanda returned to his office and handed over the photocopied pages.

"Thanks," Brett repeated. He stood up but before he and Clare left he asked, "By the way, does she have any money problems that you're aware of?"

"Huh," Ian mumbled derisively. "Doesn't every student these days?"

"Yes, but does she have *particular* financial difficulties?"

"I think you'd better ask Hannah herself, but I know she had a sizeable overdraft and had to cut some corners, to say the least. In the past few weeks it's got better, I think." He smiled cheekily and added, "I think she must have found herself a wealthy boyfriend."

Mentally, Brett added a second motive to Hannah Farr's entry on his list. Dean's money could certainly have helped to drag her out of a financial pit.

Before leaving the university campus, Brett and Clare went to the library. To get Clare through the barrier without a pass, he had to sign her in as a visitor to Mr Huxford. She did not simply vault over the security station, but she could have done so.

They had to wait for a few minutes before the Head Librarian could attend to them. When he did appear in front of them, Brett got straight to the point. "Any update on Jordan Loveday?" he queried.

"After your ... intervention, I spoke to the disciplinary committee," Mr Huxford told them. "The university's decided to suspend its action on Mr Loveday, pending further inquiries. For the moment, he's off the hook, Inspector Lawless. Thanks to you. I still think he's responsible, though, but I guess we still have to prove it."

"Well, far be it from me to tell you your business," Brett replied, "but you could leave out a valuable manuscript. Make it an easy target, but keep a close, surreptitious eye on it. Setting a trap's one option. What do you think?"

"It's dangerous, but I see your point. It would be interesting."

"It's up to you," Brett concluded, "but if you're going to make any headway, you might have to tempt your thief out into the open."

"Yes," Mr Huxford murmured. "You're probably right. I might well take up your suggestion. We'll see."

First, the graphologist put the two sheets of Hannah's handwriting on either side of the threatening letter. He squinted closely at the writing and his head moved from side to side as if he were watching a tennis match. "Mmm," he muttered. Without voicing his opinion, he took one of the transparent sheets and tried to superimpose the written words that were common to both the letter and the opening of Hannah's essay. The "and" and "the" matched almost perfectly. "Life" and "human" were just as alike. The graphologist looked up at his eager audience of two and, with a wicked expression, said, "See this phrase in the letter, 'freedom and life'? The gaps between 'freedom' and 'and' and 'and' and 'life' are the same in each document." He laughed. "Completely irrelevant to the analysis," he teased, "but it made a nice sentence. Five consecutive 'and's. Must be a record."

Brett smiled and nodded but really he wanted to hear the graphologist's opinion more than his wit. "Very droll, George," he said. "But did the same person write both documents?"

"Absolutely," George pronounced. "No doubt about it."

"OK," Brett murmured. "Good. Thanks for your help."

"I know my efforts to profile character through handwriting aren't really your cup of tea, Brett," he teased, "but, tell me, is she right-handed, young and forceful? I can see for myself from this essay that she's well educated."

Brett grinned. "OK, OK. You hit the bullseye this time – as long as she's forceful and right-handed. We'll go and find out."

Gathering up the handwriting specimens, George chirped, "I'm confident. Want a fiver on it?"

"No," Brett replied. "But I'd bet a tenner you can't get it right three times on the trot."

* * *

Brett decided to try shock tactics. He brought Hannah Farr from the university campus into the police station, put her in a drab interview room, made her stew on her own for fifteen minutes, and then went in with Clare. Businesslike, he turned on the tape recorder and reported, "Interview with Hannah Farr." He checked his watch and then continued, "The time is sixteen-twenty on Wednesday 10th January. Police officers present: Detective Sergeant Clare Tilley and Detective Inspector Brett Lawless." Finally, he glared at Hannah and said, "Some weeks ago you wrote a threatening letter to your boyfriend's father and posted it while at home in Cumbria. In the letter, you put, 'It may not always be the case that animals have a monopoly on being subjected to fatal experimentation.' Shortly after, Dr Games became ill and subsequently died. If I were you, I'd be very nervous. What do you say?"

"I don't know what you're talking about," Hannah replied, staring at him icily.

While Brett placed Hannah's letter on the desk in front of her, Clare said, for the benefit of the tape, "Detective Inspector Lawless is showing the suspect Exhibit CG3."

"Is this your writing?" Brett barked at her.

Hannah took the letter in her right hand and pretended to read through it as if she'd never seen it before. "Why do you think *I* wrote it?"

"Because it matches your writing precisely." He

thrust before her a copy of the first page of her own essay.

"I see," she retorted without a trace of remorse.

"Do you know it's an offence to make threats like this?"

"He deserves it for torturing—"

Cutting her short, Brett said, "You can't threaten to kill people – whether you agree with their politics or not. Did Dean know about this letter?"

"Dean shares my views. He has no love of his mother's or father's trade."

"Does that mean yes?"

Clare watched Hannah and said, "For the record, the suspect nodded."

"Did you kill Colin Games?" Brett asked abruptly.

"No," she stated. "But he deserved all he got."

"What about Dean?" Brett continued. "Has he been off colour at all recently? Have you noticed? Or has he complained of feeling ill?"

Hannah shrugged. "He's sulked over the odd headache, I suppose. He's been more tired than usual. He hasn't been eating so well, either. Nothing too serious, though."

"Has he given you any money recently?"

Wickedly, she answered, "He bought me a meal the other day."

"I mean, given you a substantial amount of money directly." Brett paused before adding, "Remember, we've got the power to check his financial dealings."

"I'd rather take money from a willing Dean than

from a begrudging government scheme or my family."

"What's the problem with accepting your family's help?"

"Handouts from them would mean benefiting from my dad's work at Sellafield power station. I won't have that. It's polluting the land and the sea, killing innocent creatures with its nuclear waste."

"Ultimately, hasn't Dean's money come from PHP, another company on your black list?"

"Yes," she groaned. "It's not very satisfactory but it has to come from somewhere. My dad's business is even worse than the pharmaceutical industry. Besides, now Dean's father's dead, it's one step removed from PHP."

"What about Stephanie Games?"

Hannah chuckled. "Actually, the letter was intended for her but Dean's dad opened it. *If* I'd been into killing to stop experiments on animals, I'd have gone for her first. She's closer to the cruelty."

"Your note implied that you *would* kill to achieve your aims," Brett pointed out.

"Don't you understand?" she rejoined forcefully. "A threatening letter is precisely what it says. A threat. A successful one doesn't have to be carried through."

"It wasn't successful," Brett observed. "Until his death, Colin Games was working for PHP and Stephanie Games still does. So, Hannah, what happens when a threatening letter fails? What's the next step?" He peered closely at the young woman.

"There wasn't a next step. Nothing was decided."

"Are you a member of the Campaign for Animal Rights?"

"Yes," Hannah snapped.

"Did you send similar letters to other people employed by companies that use laboratory animals?"

Hannah hesitated but decided that there was little point in denying it. "I'm proud to say I sent a few. Yes."

"Who to?" asked Clare.

"Why do you want to know?" she queried.

"Think about it. We need to check if they're still alive or whether they've met a fate similar to that of Dr Games. So, who did the others go to?"

"I can't remember."

"Come off it," Brett exclaimed. "If you refuse to tell us the other names, it could suggest you're hiding something. Are there more people like Dr Games around the country?"

"There are plenty of people like him doing horrible and pointless animal experiments."

"You know that's not what I meant," Brett said. "Have any of the ones you targeted died in mysterious circumstances?"

"No idea. As I said," she answered sweetly, "I don't remember."

"If you don't remember names of individuals on your hit list, what about the names of companies and laboratories? Where did you send those letters?"

"A couple of Medical Research Council places, Xenox, Griffin Drug House, some cosmetics manufacturers," she replied.

"OK," Brett murmured. Then he tried a different approach. "Have you ever studied science beyond your school years?" he enquired.

"No," she replied curtly. "It's science that puts bolts in monkeys' brains and induces heart attacks in dogs."

Brett might have defended his pet topic, pointing out the medical advances that were dependent on animal experiments, but he was there to investigate a motive for murder, not to start a debating society. Besides, he may not have been able to find the necessary conviction. He was convinced, though, that inflicting cruelty on humans was not the way to prevent humans inflicting cruelty on animals. "Well," he said to Hannah, "you know you've already committed a criminal act but I'm not going to charge you with an offence right now. Not until we see the outcome of a related and more serious investigation."

"I can go?"

"Soon. After we've sorted out the paperwork," Brett said. "But let me warn you: we're going to establish if you were involved in the death of Dr Colin Games before we decide what to do about you. The letter's already made you a suspect. We'll be continuing our inquiries. You'll hear from us again," he promised gravely.

Outside the interview room, Brett looked at his

watch and said to the custody officer, "Hold her for fifteen minutes. That should be enough. Then release her."

Clare smiled and queried, "A quick visit to Dean Games?"

"Definitely. Before they can talk to each other."

They found him alone at home in Dore, watching the early-evening news. He turned off the volume and invited his visitors to sit down.

"We won't be long," Brett informed him. "Just a few questions. Besides," he added, glancing at his watch, "you'll be getting a telephone call soon."

"What?" Dean asked.

"You'll find out. For the moment, I want to know why you didn't tell us that you didn't get on with your dad."

"I wasn't aware that I didn't."

"You sympathized with Hannah's threatening letter."

"Ah," Dean murmured. He examined his shoes for a few seconds before looking up again. "That was sent to Mum. I told you I don't get on with Mum. And I couldn't control Dad opening a letter for her."

Brett watched him closely and asked, "Did you kill your father, Dean?"

Dean sighed. "No. I told you –"

"Are you still feeling off colour?"

"I took your advice," Dean replied, looking towards Clare. "Went to the doctor. He said I'm suffering from stress, depression or maybe an infection. He's doing some tests."

"Was he also your father's doctor?"

"Yes."

"Did he compare your symptoms with your father's?"

Dean shook his head. "He wouldn't, would he? That would hardly be a way to cure depression, would it?"

The telephone began to ring and Brett said, "That'll be all for now, Dean. You'd better answer it. It'll be your girlfriend. We can see ourselves out."

By seven o'clock in the evening, it felt like the dead of night. The sky was as clear as a planetarium, vast and dark, punctuated by pinpoint stars. Few cars cruised the streets. The treacherous glassy pavements had been abandoned.

In the Dog and Duck, Brett gazed out of the window and said, "It looks nice – from inside." He finished his drink and murmured, "Long day."

"Yeah," Clare agreed. "Still, we're building up a clearer picture."

"Slowly," Brett commented with some frustration in his voice. "Pity we haven't got back-up. They could find out if Xenox, Griffin and the others Hannah mentioned have any cases like Colin Games. As it is, we'll have to find time to do it. Along with everything else."

"You know what else we could do?" Clare posed.

"Talk to Jordan Loveday about Hannah. They're on the same course so they may know each other quite well. Perhaps he could fill us in a bit on her character. He owes us one."

"Good idea," Brett said.

Clare put down her empty glass and remarked, "Long day tomorrow, as well, no doubt. Time to get going, I suppose."

As soon as she put a foot outside the pub, Clare skidded and toppled. Behind her, Brett set himself and then grabbed her, stopping her from falling on to the frozen tarmac of the car park. She clung to him gratefully and dragged herself upright again. Laughing at her own clumsiness, she said, "Thanks, Brett."

"OK?" he asked, letting go of her as if embarrassed to be touching her.

"Sure. Fine."

Turning it into a joke, Brett said, "It's a good job the local constabulary didn't see. You'd be breathalyzed as soon as you got into the car for being drunk and disorderly." He wouldn't admit, even to himself, that he'd enjoyed the contact with her. He'd forgotten the pleasure of holding a woman. If only it had been Zoe, he thought. He turned away, hiding his mixed emotions.

Tony Rudd extracted from the huge freezer three small vials, each containing five millilitres of frozen urine, and put them down on the table in front of Brett. "One road-accident victim, one knifing, and Colin Games's sample," he announced. "All male and in their forties. OK?"

"Thanks," Brett said. "Just what I need."

"I want the remainder back," he told Brett. "And I'll want to know any results your man gets. But I'd put my penultimate shirt on the fact that natural causes didn't get Games."

"I'll let you know as soon as I know," Brett promised. He put out his hand to take the samples but withdrew it and instead examined the three vials without touching them.

"What's wrong?" Tony and Clare asked simultaneously.

"Nothing," Brett replied. "It's just curious."

"What is?"

"Colin Games's urine is still frozen solid but the other two are melting nicely." Inside the vials, one urine sample was a yellow solid but the other two contained mini-icebergs floating in pale liquids. Almost talking to himself, Brett murmured, "Why should the two normals melt faster than Colin Games's?"

"There's probably less of them," Tony proposed. "Less thermal mass."

Brett scrutinized the contents of the vials again. "I don't think so. The three volumes are much the same. You said they were, as well."

"True," Tony responded. "If I remember my chemistry properly, what's dissolved in urine affects the temperature it melts at."

"That's right," Brett conceded. He frowned as he watched Colin Games's urine become liquid belatedly, still lagging behind the other two samples. "Maybe that's all it is," he muttered. "Different contents making different melting temperatures." But in his mind a crazy idea was forming. Too crazy to be confirmed by one unreliable observation. He could not give it any credence until he'd gathered more evidence. Hungry for further information, his visit to Derek Jacob's laboratory became even more important.

To Clare, the whole process seemed mysterious and

magical. Derek Jacob, wearing a white coat, gloves and protective spectacles, dissolved a little salt in each of the urine samples and then added a solvent that smelled sweet and fruity. It didn't mix with the watery urine but formed a clear liquid layer on top of it. Derek shook the vials vigorously and then withdrew the layer of solvent, saying, "All the organic acids that were in the urine are dissolved in here now. They prefer this solvent to water, so they moved across when I shook it. Now I've just got to derivatize them."

"*What* them?" she queried.

"As they are, the organic acids tend to decompose when you try to analyse them," Derek explained. "So, to make them suitable for the analysis I'm converting them into more co-operative chemicals. It's called derivatizing them. Clever, eh?"

"I'll take your word for it," Clare quipped.

Derek grinned. "It'll take half an hour. Why don't you treat me to a coffee while we wait?"

In the bustling coffee bar, Derek kept an eye on his watch. "Do you know how much I'd charge you for this analysis if you were in industry?" he asked them.

"Some exorbitant price," Brett suggested.

"Too right. The going rate would be about two hundred pounds." He shook his head. "I'm a sucker for the local constabulary. I'm a sucker for curiosity."

"Well, I've got some good news for you," Brett announced. "I got a bit of a budget from the Forensic Department. No money, I'm afraid, but if you give me the details of something you need for your lab – up to a value of a hundred – we'll buy it for you. How's that?"

"Back to the days of bartering!" Derek exclaimed with a chuckle. "I like it. I thought I'd get nothing but a get-out-of-jail-free card for the next time I'm caught speeding."

They returned to the laboratory when the reaction in each of the three tubes was complete. "Right. The moment of truth," Derek proclaimed. With a syringe, he took a minute amount of one of the two normal samples and injected it into the GC/MS system where the gas chromatograph would separate all of the substances in the urine and the mass spectrometer would identify them. After a while, the screen of the controlling computer began to fill with peaks, one for each substance. To Clare, it was as meaningless as hieroglyphics but Brett and Derek huddled over the results and seemed satisfied that they were as expected. Next, Derek injected Colin Games's sample and Clare noticed Brett go tense. She guessed that he had a private theory and that he expected the experiment to confirm or deny it.

This time, Derek seemed more hesitant and thoughtful as he examined the developing results. "This peak," he said, pointing to a fat one on the screen, "is strange. I can tell from its position and shape that it's due to urea. That's not important – urea's the major component of everyone's urine – but its mass is –" He paused before adding, "That's a nuisance. The instrument must have gone out of calibration."

"Why do you say that?" asked Brett.

"Well, after derivatization, urea would have a mass of 204. This is showing 205 and 206. There are other anomalies too. Many of these substances in his urine appear to be one or two mass units greater than they should be. Your man might've been ill but illness can only affect the type and quantity of urine components. It can't affect the masses of the molecules. Nature fixes those. It's got to be an instrumental error."

Clare only had to glance at Brett to know that he disagreed. He was practically oozing excitement. He almost seemed to expect the unusual results.

"You could try the last sample," Brett said animatedly. "If the system's playing up, the results will be just as weird. If it's something to do with our victim's urine, the next will be normal again."

"Indeed they will," Derek agreed. "OK. Let's do that. I'm glad police work hasn't blunted your brain altogether."

Clare watched them. They were like a couple of enthusiastic boys, experimenting with a new toy. A chemistry set for Christmas, perhaps. One thrilled that the plaything was behaving oddly, the other convinced that it had broken. She would have laughed aloud at them but she sensed from Brett's manner that the next few minutes were crucial. She had learnt to respect his judgement when it came to facts and theories.

When he viewed the next set of results, Derek inhaled sharply. "These are normal again!" he exclaimed. He turned to Brett and said, "Do you know something I don't?"

"No," Brett replied. "But I've got an idea. Let's have another look at the data for the important sample." Once Derek had re-called Colin Games's results to the monitor, Brett asked, "Forget the funny masses for the moment. What do you think of the profile in general?"

"It's all over the place. This peak here should be tiny but it's huge. This one, though," he said, indicating a hardly visible response, "should be large in a normal sample. Your man's got a massive imbalance in his body chemistry. I've never seen such disruption. But I don't know what caused it."

Brett was almost exploding with the thrill of his discovery, whatever it was. "OK," he said. "I think there's an explanation of the change in mass, and it's nothing to do with the instrument. What if the urine was a mixture of water and heavy water?"

"Heavy water?" Derek uttered. For a moment he was silent as he pondered on Brett's suggestion. "Yes. I see what you mean. That would do it. The mass of the urea derivative would be 205 or 206 depending on how much heavy water was in there. But..." His voice trailed away.

Clare butted in, saying, "Excuse my ignorance. What are we saying here? Can you speak in English?"

Derek answered Clare's question first. "Your

partner's saying something almost incredible. He's saying your victim's been given heavy water instead of the real, normal stuff. Heavy water looks exactly the same as normal water. No one would be able to tell the difference but the body would react very badly to it." Slipping into lecturer mode, he continued, "Water's H_2O – it's made of two parts hydrogen and one part oxygen. In heavy water, the hydrogen's replaced with deuterium – that's just a heavier version of hydrogen, but otherwise identical to it: D_2O. In the body, the deuterium would get incorporated into most of the body chemicals instead of hydrogen. Because deuterium's one mass unit greater than hydrogen, everything appearing in your man's urine is coming out heavier than it should."

"And," Brett added, "if I remember rightly, heavy water has a higher melting temperature than normal water. That's why the urine took a bit longer to melt."

"Yes," the professor confirmed. "It's a few degrees higher. But I don't know why we're doing all this speculating. I can check it in a couple of minutes. All I have to do is leak some of the original urine into the instrument. Normal water has a mass of eighteen. Heavy water's twenty. A mass spectrometer will distinguish them."

Engrossed, Clare watched as the two men dashed to fetch the urine sample as if they'd just thought of a new game to play with their fancy toy.

Derek injected the urine into a different part of the

instrument and, with Brett, fixed his attention avidly on the screen, waiting impatiently for the result to appear.

Suddenly, both of them let out a mutual cheer. "Spot on!" Brett cried.

Infected by their exuberance, Clare appeared between them. "Case proved?" she enquired.

"Yes," Brett answered. "The water in his urine is actually a mixture of water and heavy water."

"And that can't happen naturally?" Clare questioned.

"No," Derek concluded. "I'd say you've got yourselves an utterly remarkable case of poisoning. Heavy water would explain your long list of symptoms, as well. You see," Derek explained to Clare, "what you have here is a case of deceit. Deceitful water. Your man's been fed on heavy water and his body's been deceived by it. Normal water and heavy water are so similar that his cells didn't spot the difference. Unwittingly, they welcomed the heavy water in with open arms. It's successfully masqueraded as normal water but it's toxic. Once in, the counterfeit water's gone about its business of wreaking havoc throughout his body. It's so cunning and bizarre I never thought of it before."

"A mole in the system," Brett mused. "A very destructive one."

"Nasty," Derek murmured. "Murder by water."

"Or suicide?" Clare proposed.

"I doubt it," Brett answered. "Someone's gone to

great lengths to make sure the cause of death's almost undetectable. The usual tests can't distinguish between water and heavy water. The two are virtually identical, except to a mass spectrometer. Suicides don't worry about disguising their deaths. And heavy water's such an unlikely choice of weapon. They go for certainty more than subtlety."

"Is this heavy water easy to get hold of?" asked Clare.

"To most people, no," Derek said. "But, to a chemist, it's a doddle. Several manufacturers make it in bulk. It's used as a coolant and moderator in some types of nuclear reactor. Chemists and biochemists use it for a number of studies, especially as a solvent in an analytical method called NMR. So, getting it's no problem. I agree with Brett. Unlikely as it seems, you've got yourselves a murderer who knows some extremely devious chemistry and who's got access to chemicals."

"Thanks, Derek," Brett said. "You've come up trumps again. Great stuff."

Clare and Brett left the department with a handful of hard copy and a murder case to solve.

"Back to the library, then," Brett commented as they left the chemistry block.

"For more on Jordan Loveday?" Clare queried. She expected her partner to have more important matters on his mind.

"No. For more on heavy water."

Clare had never been in a library so much since she started working with Brett. In an investigation, she relied on her understanding of people while Brett relied on an endless supply of facts and figures. Still, he got results.

When Brett had signed in Clare and they'd entered the building, Lynne Freestone's accusing eyes followed them until they were out of her sight. The Assistant Librarian made them feel like mischievous students who were about to defile her hallowed patch. They did their best to ignore her. After searching through the library's database, Brett headed for the reference section. "It'll be in this chemical encyclopaedia," he whispered, plucking a tattered book from the shelf and running down the list of contents. "Here we go. There's a section on deuterium. Listen to this: 'Living organisms can use heavy water in place of normal water as long as the amount is below a quarter of the total water. Replacement of more than a third of the body's hydrogen by deuterium has catastrophic consequences.' Ah, it gets better. 'In mice and rats, heavy water results in sterility, a tendency to convulsions, anaemia and kidney failure. The aquarium fish, the black-lined tetra, is not affected by five per cent heavy water but shows immediate distress in forty per cent D_2O. After drastic internal disruption of all functions, it survives for a maximum of ten days.'" Brett looked up from the page and whispered, "That's a shame, experimenting on tetras – they're one of my favourite fish." Reading again, he muttered, "'In dogs, D_2O causes a decrease in blood glucose, haemoglobin and red-blood-cell count.' Sounds familiar, eh?"

Among the huge tomes that were stacked to the ceiling, Clare nodded. "We'd better go and report to the Chief."

On the way back to the car and headquarters, Brett asked, "Do you know how much water there is in a human body?"

"No," she answered.

"A lot. It's about three-quarters of our body weight. If about half of Colin Games's water was heavy water, that was an awful lot. It's not just a one-off dose that's been fed to him."

"No accident, then," Clare deduced.

"No. He's been poisoned slowly. Over a period of days or even weeks."

"But wouldn't he have known he was drinking the wrong sort of water?"

"No. They look the same. Heavy water tastes much the same as well – a bit insipid, that's all. But if it was made into tea, coffee, squash or whatever – or if it was given to him as a mixture with normal water – it certainly wouldn't be noticeable."

"If he was given heavy water in his drinks over a period, it implies he was poisoned at home or at work – the only places where he'd drink regularly."

"Yes," Brett replied. "We need to search his house for traces of D_2O. We need to know the drinking arrangement at PHP. And we need to know how much heavy water PHP buys. Xenox as well – just in case – but I don't know how they'd make sure he drank it. And remember Hannah's dad? He works at a nuclear-power plant. Access to lots of heavy water there. The question is, did his daughter get any of it?"

"Do you think we'll get a team now we've got a murder?"

Brett shook his head and smiled ruefully. "We should. We need it now we've got so much to do. But you know what I think he'll say? 'Short on resources, and you've done so well getting this far on your own, I think you should carry on as you are.' Penalized by success."

Clare laughed. "You're probably right."

Detective Chief Superintendent Keith Johnstone scanned Brett's report and then looked up at his detectives. "Well done, both of you. This is good work. Very good. No one else would've cracked it. You know, I think you're doing such a good job as you are, a team would only get in your way. Hold you back. I think you work best just as a pair – not encumbered by having to organize a team. Carry on!"

"How about an assistant, sir?" Brett argued. "Someone who can chase round after facts while we get on with the meat of the inquiry. A researcher. If we don't have one, we're not going to be able to deliver very quickly."

The Chief deliberated on Brett's passionate

request. "OK," he decided. "I'll release Liz from her current duties. She's good at what you've got in mind."

"Agreed," Brett replied. He'd worked with Liz before. She was a good officer. "Thank you, sir."

"Just one thing. Now I've been generous, I expect you to reel in the perpetrator pretty quickly."

Calling together his slightly enlarged team, Brett briefed Liz. He ended up saying, "Right now, Clare and I should concentrate on PHP while it's still normal working hours. We'll speak to Stephanie Games while we're there, if she's back at work. Liz, I've got a million things for you to do, I'm afraid. Enough for an entire team and a dozen phones."

"So what's new?" she retorted with a grin.

Brett urged her to probe the nuclear-power station where Mr Farr worked. He wanted to know if the power plant had lost any heavy water recently. He also asked her to check if any supplier had noted a sudden increase in purchases of heavy water by PHP or Xenox, or if there had been any unusual deaths among scientists associated with animal experiments at Medical Research Council laboratories, the major cosmetics manufacturers, Xenox, and Griffin Drug House. "Then there's the Games's place," he added. "Can you explain to a forensic team what we're looking for and get them round to the house tonight, when Stephanie and Dean are there? Samples of water from taps, tanks, outside barrels, anywhere.

That's what they need to test."

"And we need an address for a student called Jordan Loveday," Clare put in. "Don't forget I want to speak to him about Hannah Farr," she said to Brett. "He might be a good source."

Brett nodded. "OK. At least that's not difficult. His details will be on file. He was arrested on Sunday. Threatening behaviour. He'll be out on bail. Phone his address through when you've got it. We might be able to drop in on him tonight as well."

"All right," Liz replied playfully. "You two go out and enjoy yourselves. Grab some glory. I'll just sit here alone with my phone."

Brett smiled at her. "Thanks, Liz. You'll love it really. Welcome aboard Operation Deep Water."

Clare and Brett were steered into the familiar decorative meeting room at PHP where they waited for Stephanie Games. As soon as she joined them, she asked, "Have you got some news?"

Brett nodded. "Yes. I'm afraid so. Take a seat." Gently, he said, "I have to tell you that your husband did not die from natural causes. He was murdered."

"Murdered?" she exclaimed. "But … how?"

"He was poisoned, over a prolonged period," Brett answered factually.

"But who –?"

"Do *you* have any suggestions?" asked Clare.

Stephanie rolled her eyes as if she were in pain or baffled. "No. I don't know. I can't… What was he poisoned with? It must have been something unusual or I'd have recognized the symptoms."

"Very unusual," Brett admitted. "I can say only that it was something in the water."

Stephanie's mouth opened in surprise. Before she spoke, though, she swallowed. "That means he was poisoned here at work," she concluded eagerly.

"Why do you say that?" Brett enquired.

"Because, well, there aren't any poisons at home. And I'm not ill, am I?"

"What about Dean?"

She hesitated and then answered, "His dad's death has just got him down a bit, that's all."

Brett didn't tell her that a forensic team would examine her house that evening. He didn't want to forewarn her because, if she was guilty of murder, she would have an opportunity to get rid of any incriminating evidence. Brett ended the interview by suggesting that the pathologist would probably release Colin's body soon, now that his death had been clarified.

His widow muttered, "Oh well. That's one good thing, I suppose."

After Stephanie Games had left them, Clare delivered her assessment of the biologist. "She was genuinely surprised," Clare whispered. "But it doesn't help us a lot. If she killed her husband, she used heavy water to disguise the murder. She'd be amazed that you cracked it. So, surprise if she's guilty, surprise if she's innocent."

They stood and strolled around the room, waiting impatiently for ten minutes before a reluctant Dr Raynor appeared.

As he entered the room, Kelvin Raynor adjusted his spectacles on his nose and then fiddled with his tie. He seemed uncomfortable. He invited the detectives to sit down. He was less intimidated by their height when they were seated. "What can I do for you?" he asked politely.

"We won't take up much of your time," Brett began, "but there's a couple of things you may be able to help us with. For instance, did you see Colin Games speaking to Paul Dunnett at the London conference last November?"

"Er..." Kelvin was caught unawares by the unexpected question. "Paul Dunnett. He's from Xenox. Right?"

"Right," Brett confirmed. "He attended that conference in London, along with Colin Games and you."

"Yes, but what would they have to speak about?"

Brett shrugged. "Business in general. The weather. University days. Apparently they were at university together. But that's not the point. Did you see them together?"

"No," he answered, fidgeting in his chair.

Clare guessed that he was lying.

"OK," Brett continued. "I'd like to know if PHP uses much heavy water."

"Heavy water? Well, yes. Our analytical department uses quite a bit. Why?"

Ignoring the question, Brett said, "We'll need to see your orders for the past few months."

"I don't know," Dr Raynor replied hesitantly. "Such things are kept to ourselves. We have to protect our usage of chemicals from competitors because they could deduce some of our activities if they knew that information."

"I'm not a competitor," Brett stated bluntly. "I'm a police officer investigating the murder of one of your employees. So I *will* see those orders."

Kelvin looked stunned. "Murder!" Then he sighed with resignation. "I see. In that case, I'd better ask Mr Schulten to come and see you."

"Only he has the authority to open up the order books, I suppose?" Brett responded.

"That's right."

"OK. But before you do that, let me ask you a last question. What arrangements did Colin Games have for morning and afternoon breaks?"

"He took coffee in an office adjoining his laboratory," answered Kelvin. "Obviously, eating and drinking isn't allowed in the lab itself, for safety reasons, but he didn't like to leave the lab area and walk to the tea room. He always said he was too busy."

"Did anyone join him for coffee?"

"Just his technician, I think. Simon Mortimer. It was a two-man outfit. Simon always worked closely with Colin."

"Then we'll need to see Mr Mortimer as well," Brett concluded.

"I'm not sure—"

Interrupting, Brett said, "Let's face it. We'll see him here and now or, if you don't approve, at home this evening when it's out of your control. So let's have him in now, please."

Dr Raynor relented. "I'll get Simon," he proclaimed, "so you can speak to him while I go and consult Mr Schulten."

As soon as he'd left the meeting room, Brett said quietly to Clare, "Our Dr Raynor was lying, wasn't he? He *did* see something at that conference."

Clare smiled. "You're getting the hang of this job. Mind you, his body language wasn't exactly subtle. I'd say he thought that Dr Games and Paul Dunnett were conspiring together. That means he's got a motive – even if Dunnett's telling the truth when he said that Games turned him down."

A few minutes later, Dr Raynor brought in Colin Games's technician. Simon Mortimer was all arms, legs and teeth. He was thin, immensely tall and equipped with a full set of protruding teeth like a horse. When he opened his mouth, he always seemed to be smiling. But he wasn't.

Brett waved him towards a chair while Kelvin Raynor slipped out again. "Thanks for coming in," Brett said. "We'd like to talk to you because you were Dr Games's technician, I've been told."

"Technician! Slave's more like it."

"So you didn't get on?"

"I wouldn't say that," the forthright technician replied, showing his large, white teeth. "We had to get on. Otherwise, life in the lab would've been even worse. But we were colleagues, not friends."

"Did he have any enemies?" Brett enquired.

"He didn't have many friends," Simon answered. "A loner, he was." The technician rested his long arms on the table. They reached almost halfway across it. With the fingers of his right hand he fiddled with a cheap and chewed biro. He was in his thirties and on top of his head there was a large, round bald patch. He was so lanky that it would have been well out of sight if he'd been standing up.

"Had you worked with Colin Games for long?"

"A couple of years."

"And before that?"

"Oh, a succession of short-term contracts, all over the place. I've been in the food industry, a school laboratory, environmental monitoring of water supplies, the hospital. Two years is long term to me."

"What did you do for tea and coffee breaks here? Take them with Colin Games?"

"Yeah. We brewed up in the office," he muttered.

"You sound as if you were fed up with that arrangement," Clare observed.

"Let me be honest," Simon responded, tapping his pen on the surface of the table. "He treated me like dirt. I'm a qualified chemist, you know, but he gave me all the trivial jobs. Seemed to think that was my limit. Running his errands, making his starting materials, cleaning up the lab. And he never trusted me with information on his target products. Kept the final structures to himself. All told, I would've rather been somewhere else for breaks."

"So," Brett mused, "there's a drinking-water tap in the office?"

"Yes."

"And who made the coffee?"

"Either of us."

"I see," Brett murmured.

"Did anyone else come in and make any drinks?" Clare interjected.

"Yes. His wife would join us sometimes. Quite a lot in his last few weeks."

"Interesting. Did Colin ever have coffee or anything with Kelvin Raynor or Mr Schulten?" Brett queried.

"Occasionally. That's all."

"So you drank the same drinks as Dr Games?"

Simon nodded.

"Have you been ill at all recently?"

Using a strange but appropriate simile, he replied, "Healthy as a horse, me." He paused before asking, "You don't think there was something in the water, do you? That's not possible. If there was, I'd have copped it as well."

"We're keeping an open mind," Brett fibbed. "Anyway, what's your position in the company now?"

"Technical assistant to Dr Raynor's group."

"Is that better for you than before?"

"I don't like to profit by anyone's death but, yes, it is."

"OK, Simon," Brett concluded. "That's it for now. You've been very helpful."

"Have I?" he murmured as he stood.

"Yes," Brett and Clare replied.

The towering technician bent his neck to avoid cracking his head on the door frame as he went out.

"Bet he's good at basketball," Clare remarked with a smirk.

"He could be good at poisoning as well," Brett said. "He'd got a motive – he disliked his boss quite a bit. And clearly he's got the chemical knowledge, as well as the opportunity. At breaks, perhaps he made the drinks more than he admitted. He could've brewed up with heavy water for Games and used tap water for himself. We've got ourselves another suspect to add to the list."

"Yes, but he didn't try to hide his dislike of Colin Games," Clare protested. "Seems the plain-speaking honest Yorkshire type to me."

"Not much point in him denying the clash when he knew we'd discover it through Kelvin Raynor or Stephanie Games. He could be sincere *and* a killer. A sort of double bluff. Perhaps he thinks murderers always disguise their hatred for their victims, so he was open about it."

"All right. I admit there's a possibility," said Clare.

Brett's mobile phone began to trill just as Kelvin Raynor came back into the room with Mr Schulten. "Excuse me," Brett said and answered the call.

It was Liz. She gave him Jordan Loveday's address

in Broomhill and then reported the outcome of her vexed conversations with Nuclear Products. "They're not admitting to missing *anything*," she informed him. "A bunch of clams. Their policy seems to be to deny anything and everything."

"All right," Brett replied. "Forget it for now. See if you have better luck with the next jobs: chasing up suppliers and the personnel at the other companies." He thanked her and rang off. Turning towards Mr Schulten, Brett said, "Sorry about that. I'm grateful you could come and see us."

Not wasting time, Mr Schulten declared, "I understand you want to see our requisitions of heavy water."

"Yes," Brett announced, not volunteering an explanation.

"Why?"

Immune to Mr Schulten's prompting, Brett responded, "Because it will aid our investigation of Colin Games's murder."

"I don't know how."

"No, but you wouldn't want to obstruct that inquiry, I'm sure. You'll be as anxious as us to find out who was responsible for the death of one of your valued employees. If it was someone here at PHP you'd certainly want us to make an arrest, before you lose another worker. On top of that, I can – and if necessary will – get an order to force you to hand over the information."

Mr Schulten gazed at Brett for a moment, assessing

his resolve. "All right," he conceded begrudgingly. "It's not the most sensitive of the chemicals we order. But the details aren't immediately to hand. I'll ask our laboratory superintendent to search out the relevant information and have it faxed to you tomorrow."

"All right," Brett agreed. "Thanks for your co-operation."

As Clare and Brett were leaving the car park at PHP, Liz called again. She announced, "You've got a visitor here. A Hannah Farr wants to speak to you. She won't talk to me."

Brett was intrigued. "OK. Tell her to wait. We won't be long. We'll come in before we go to Loveday's place."

Hannah was sitting in Interview Room Four. She had undone her coat but had not taken it off. Clearly, she didn't intend to stay for long. Confirming it in words, she rose and pronounced, "Don't bother to sit down. I only want to tell you something, then I'm off. You've kept me waiting long enough already."

"Sorry to detain you," Brett commented. "What did you want to say to us?"

"It's Dean. He's playing it down but he's getting quite sick. Nausea. Off his food and tired all the time. I thought you ought to know. Before, I said it was nothing serious but it's getting worse and I'm getting worried. It's not that different from how his dad started." She stared at Brett significantly.

"Thanks for letting us know," Brett said. "Rest

assured, we're looking into all the possibilities, and we're taking Dean's health into account."

"Good," she uttered and strode towards the door.

"Before you go," Brett said, stopping Hannah in her tracks, "do you know much about your dad's business?"

"Enough," she snapped.

"Enough for what?"

"Enough to know I don't want to know any more. The nuclear industry's a blight on the country, and on the planet."

"What coolant does his reactor use?" enquired Brett.

Hannah frowned. "Coolant? No idea. I don't want to know that much."

"OK." Brett relented and let her escape. "Thanks for taking the trouble to tell us about Dean." Once she'd left, Brett asked Clare, "Is that a concerned girlfriend – or an attempt to manipulate us?"

Clare smiled. "Possibly a concerned girlfriend. Definitely a manipulator."

Brett nodded. "Gives us something to think about while we go and have a word with Jordan Loveday. See what he knows about her."

Jordan occupied a ground-floor bedsit in a rickety old house in Broomhill, not far from the university. Clare and Brett stood in the cold, draughty hall, banged on his door and waited. Nothing happened. They knocked loudly again. From inside, there came a distinct clatter but the door remained closed.

"Well..." Brett began. He stopped talking when the front door opened and Jordan Loveday walked into the hall rubbing his hands. Brett called to him quickly, "Jordan, is anyone in your room?"

The student stopped and stared at the two detectives. "You!" he exclaimed.

"Is there supposed to be anyone in?" Brett repeated urgently.

Jordan shook his head. "No."

"Is there another way out?"

"No. Not unless you count the big window at the back. Don't tell me I'm being burgled! Not on top of—"

Brett interrupted him, asking, "Presumably you've got a key?" Seeing him nod, Brett said to his partner, "You stay here with Jordan. Give me two minutes to get round the back. Then you go in while I'm covering the window."

Clare nodded and Brett dashed back outside. To the left, along the side of the house, there was a narrow path leading to the bare concrete yard where snow had piled up along the tall back wall. Brett squinted cautiously into the darkened area. There was an outhouse, some tubs that in summer were probably alive with flowers, the front wheel of a bicycle and a big dustbin. Everything was quiet. It was easy to locate Jordan's window. It had been smashed and some shards of glass glinted on the ground. Noiselessly, Brett crept up to it and listened. He could not hear anything from inside. He waited to one side of the window, steeling himself to tackle the intruder if he fled through the broken window when Clare crashed into the room.

Brett heard the key in the lock and, immediately after, the door bursting open. The light came on behind the curtain and a bright yellow rectangle appeared on the wall. From inside, Clare called, "No one here!"

Puzzled, Brett swung round. By the new light, he saw the dustbin briefly before it hit him, thrown by someone who must have been hiding behind it. Luckily, there was not much rubbish inside so it was not very heavy, but it caught him across the stomach and winded him. Brett took a few breaths to recover his composure and then pushed away the dustbin with his foot. "He's out here!" Brett shouted to Clare. "I'm going after him." Brett dashed down the path after the prowler. In the moment before he'd been struck, Brett had seen only the missile, not the face of the intruder. He hadn't even gathered whether the heavily dressed figure that had dashed out of the yard was male or female.

By the time that Brett emerged on to the street, the burglar was sprinting down the road, well ahead of him. Brett took another deep gasp of sharp air, searing his throat and lungs. Then he took off. It wasn't easy to run fast and securely on the frozen pavement. He had to slow down at each crossroads in case of traffic and to make sure that he didn't slip over at the snowbound kerbs. In front of him, the burglar, belching clouds, turned left and out of sight. By the time that Brett reached the same corner and stared down the avenue, it seemed to be deserted. It was a short street, connecting two more major roads. There were perhaps twenty houses on each side of the road, the bare skeletons of regularly spaced trees, quite a few parked cars, a telephone kiosk and a post box. His quarry could be hiding almost anywhere.

Slowly and silently, Brett walked down one side of the road, looking carefully into each garden and behind each car as he went. Unfortunately, there was not enough snow on the pavement to follow the burglar's footprints but Brett scrutinized each lawn for fresh impressions. Suddenly, there was a noise from the next garden. Brett stiffened and waited. Nothing. The noise had stopped. He took two or three more tentative paces and there was another sound from the same place. Then a black cat jumped over the low wall of the garden and slinked guiltily across his path. Brett grimaced and continued his search.

A couple of cars appeared briefly as they travelled gently along the main road but they shunned the eerily quiet avenue. The telephone kiosk was empty and no one was hiding behind the post box. Brett hesitated when he caught the distant sound of a squad-car siren. Obviously, Clare had called for back-up. They would help at the house but they were too late to assist Brett. He reached the end of the road, crossed over and began to make his way back on the other side, again examining gardens and any other hiding places. He even ducked down and looked into the inky space beneath each car.

As soon as he dropped down and peered under the second car, feeling the ice-cold water seeping uncomfortably into his trousers at the knee, he heard another car being started and its engine revving up ferociously. Brett sprang to his feet. At the top of the street, the last in the line of parked cars roared into life. The driver's door opened slightly and then slammed shut. Presumably on purpose, the lights were left off. The car pulled away but almost immediately its tyres spun ineffectually because the driver had pumped too hard on the accelerator. The car skidded, slid backwards and sideways against the kerb, jolted, and only then found a grip. Brett ran towards it as fast as he could but slipped and found himself flat on his back. All he saw from his prostrate position on the paving stones was the outline of the car turning on to the main road and disappearing. He was too far away to read the registration number. He couldn't even identify the model or the colour for sure. He knew only that it was a dark saloon car, possibly deep blue. The intruder must have dived into the car immediately on entering the street and then laid low until Brett reached the far end of the avenue. At first, the driver hadn't even closed the door in case Brett had been alerted by the click.

Brett cursed to himself and trudged back empty-handed to Jordan Loveday's flat. Cheerlessly, he flashed his warrant card at the uniformed officer standing by the door and mumbled, "DI Lawless."

Inside, Clare asked, "Well?"

Brett shook his head and sighed. "Lost him. Didn't even get a good look at him – or her – or the car."

Clare glanced at her partner from head to foot and remarked, "Heavy dry-cleaning bill today."

Brett glanced down and noted for the first time how the encounter had soiled his clothes. "I'll present the bill to the Chief," he quipped. Then he turned his attention to the bedsit and asked Clare and Jordan, "Well? What's been going on here?"

Clare replied, "Jordan doesn't seem to think anything's missing." She hesitated before continuing, "Brett, you must have seen plenty of burglaries when you were in uniform. Does this look typical to you?"

Brett surveyed the room. "No. They were mainly clumsy kids emptying drawers and cupboards after computer games, anything small enough to carry off easily, like cash and credit cards. If it was vandals, there'd be scrawling on the walls, the front room used as a toilet. That sort of thing." Brett cast his eyes round again. "Nothing like that here."

"Quite," Clare replied. "This looks too polite – or half-hearted. The tidiest break-in I've seen. No scrawls. A few things moved and knocked over but nothing broken. A couple of drawers have been opened but the contents have only been disturbed, not dragged out hastily. Hardly an efficient rummage. And nothing stolen apparently."

"We did disturb him," Brett noted.

"Even so, there should be more mess."

"I know. I'm not sure what we're dealing with here. Are you, Jordan?"

Jordan merely shrugged. He was still shocked and annoyed.

"Let's take a look around, then," Brett suggested. "No touching anything till they've got all the prints they want. And watch out for broken glass."

Some books had been cast from their shelves and lay on the floor. Cassette tapes had been shuffled and dislodged. A small computer pocket-book remained on Jordan's desk but the pens and paper had been scattered on to the carpet. "Bit of a token gesture of a burglary," Brett murmured. "Portable computers are the first thing to disappear."

"Look," Clare said, waving them towards one of the half-open drawers.

An old manuscript could just be seen among the jumpers and socks. Brett looked at Jordan and asked, "What's that?"

Jordan's face expressed anguish and anger. "No idea! Never seen it before," he claimed.

"So you've never touched it?" Clare put in.

"Of course not."

"OK," Brett said. He turned and shouted for the forensic scientist. "Prints on that book, if you will," he requested. "Priority." Addressing Jordan again, he enquired, "I suppose you had your fingerprints taken on Sunday, didn't you?"

"Yes." Aggressively, he added, "And you won't find them on that book!"

"Good," Brett replied. "Because if we do, you'll be in big trouble. If your prints *aren't* there, it won't confirm anything – a cautious thief would use gloves – but it'll certainly help your cause."

"How *do* you account for the book being here?" Clare asked him.

He shrugged. "Wasn't there this morning when I

got this jumper out," he said, yanking the front of his pullover.

"You're saying someone's pretended to burgle you to plant a stolen book on you?" Brett queried.

"Must have."

Brett asked the gloved forensic scientist to open the book. Inside the front cover there was the university's insignia and a label with big bold lettering: **Not to be removed from the library**.

"Mmm," Brett murmured thoughtfully.

"You don't believe me, do you?" Jordan cried.

"The jury's still out," Brett replied sceptically. "But I must admit this isn't a very convincing robbery – even considering that we disturbed the burglar."

"If it's any consolation," Clare added, "I believe you."

Jordan's eyes moved from Brett to Clare and back again. He seemed to be assessing them. Then in a conciliatory tone he said, "I'm sorry I slagged you off in the police station. The university told me I'm off the hook for the moment. I gathered it was something you did."

"There's a lot of evidence against you but I pointed out a weakness in it, that's all," Brett told him. "I didn't have anything definite to say about guilt or innocence. I still don't – yet."

"Yeah. Well, it won't matter now. When they find out about this," he moaned, nodding towards the book, "I'll be suspended again, then sent down."

"Not necessarily," Brett rejoined. "You can refer the university to us. We can tell them there are two ways this book could have arrived here. Either you nicked it or your unconvincing burglar planted it on you. The book's no proof."

"I hope they listen to you but I doubt it," Jordan responded, groaning pessimistically.

"Look, I hate to belittle your problems, but we've got ours as well," Brett confessed. "You might have wondered what we were doing here. We came to ask you a question. Do you know Hannah Farr? She's on your course."

"Hannah?" he answered. "Yeah, sure. She's in my tutorial group. Why?"

"What's she like?" Brett asked.

"She's OK. What do you mean?"

"Do you know if she's interested in animal rights?"

Jordan laughed. "Interested? You're not kidding. I don't think she's interested in anything else."

"How far do you think she'd go in protesting about animal experiments? Do you think she'd use violence?"

"Hannah? Violent? No. She wouldn't hurt a fly. If one had to be swatted, she'd have to get someone else to do it for her."

"Flies aren't the issue," Brett retorted with a grin. "I'm sure any animal is safe from her. But what about human beings – particularly ones who might be cruel to animals?"

Jordan considered it for a second. "She gets heated about it, sure," he answered, "but I don't think she'd hurt anything or anyone. She's just not the type." He looked at Clare and added, "I dare say you're not going to tell me what this is all about."

"You're right. We're not," Clare replied pleasantly. "But we'll do what we can for you over this library business. Try to get to the bottom of it."

"Thanks," Jordan said appreciatively.

"But for now," Brett put in, "we've got to crack on. We'll leave you in the hands of this crew," he said, indicating the uniformed officers. "They'll finish soon but I'm afraid they're not sufficiently house-trained to clear up afterwards. That's your job. They'll give you the telephone number of an emergency glazier who'll fit a new window pronto. There's so many burglaries round here, they know it off by heart."

As Clare drove away, Brett said, "Let's not go too far. I want to drop in at the university library for a couple of minutes. See if Mr Huxford's still there. If he is, I'll check out that book."

"OK," said Clare, indicating right to take the road back to the university site.

Clare waited outside while Brett used his pass to get into the library again. The enquiry desk was quiet. Only Mr Huxford and Lynne Freestone were on duty. Avoiding Lynne's stare, Brett asked Mr Huxford if he had taken any action to trap the thief.

"Yes," he reported grimly. "I took your advice. And I'm not at all happy about it. The book disappeared today! It attracted our culprit all right but he got away with it – even though Mrs Freestone and I kept an eye on it. I was about to contact you to report it missing, to see if you could organize a search because," he added meaningfully, "Loveday *was* in the library this morning."

Brett checked that the volume he'd seen in Jordan's room was the missing book.

"So," the Head Librarian cried, "you've found it already. What a relief! Where was it?"

Brett admitted, "Exactly where you'd expect, I'm afraid. Mr Loveday's place."

"That's it, then," Mr Huxford surmised. "We've got him."

"Let's not be hasty," Brett replied. "It'd still be premature – and unwise – to assume he's guilty. Yes, he could have stolen it, but somebody who just broke into his flat could have left the book there. On purpose. To incriminate him. I want to interview that burglar. I'm asking you – and the university – not to condemn Jordan Loveday until I've completed my inquiries regarding this burglary."

"Well," Mr Huxford said, hesitating, "I'll do my best. But, you must agree, it looks bad. And this conspiracy idea seems a bit far-fetched. At least that's how the disciplinary committee will see it. However," he pronounced, "I'll present your … charitable view to the committee as best I can."

"Thank you, Mr Huxford," Brett said. "I'll make sure Forensics return the book to you as soon as possible. And they'll need your fingerprints to eliminate them from any that they find on the book."

The Head Librarian grimaced momentarily but replied, "Distasteful, but I understand the need."

Back in the car, Clare glanced at her partner and commented, "You look knackered."

"No. Not really. Not physically tired. A bit weary, though. And I'm annoyed with myself for losing that intruder. If I'd got him, we might've cleared this library thing up by now. There's something else as well. Something else that gets to me. It's deceit, I suppose. First, we get deceitful water. Now, I might just have witnessed deceit in the library."

"Oh?"

"Jordan's always been in the library when something goes missing. Twenty times. Twenty-one now. *If* he's innocent, that's an amazing coincidence."

"Not if someone's targeted him to take the blame," Clare said, thoughtfully.

"Quite. And who's in a position to know when he goes into the library – and make sure that the thieving only occurs during one of his visits?"

"A member of staff," Clare suggested.

"Right. A member of staff. And what's gone missing is the book that Huxford left out as a trap. That puts him in a good position to orchestrate this whole business. I guess it could be any of the staff – like Lynne Freestone who was also supposed to be keeping watch on the target book – but it strikes me that, if Jordan didn't do it, Huxford's the linchpin."

"You think Huxford's behind it, earning something on the side by stealing and selling the library's best books, then blaming it on a student?"

"Yes. It's a real possibility. Depressing if it's true. Students have it tough enough without being framed for the staff's misdemeanours. No wonder Jordan Loveday cracked."

"What are you going to do about it? It's not our job, of course. The Chief'll go ballistic if we take time out of a murder investigation for it. Same thing if you get Liz to dig around. We didn't get her for probing scams with library books."

"I know. It's tricky. But there's something she could do without damaging the Games case." Brett watched Clare take a left turn and asked, "Where are we going, Clare?"

"My place," she answered. "I've taken it upon myself to sort you out. I'll treat you to some real ale and a chilli. Make you feel better. Yes?"

Brett hesitated, but then relented and smiled. "OK. Thanks. That'll be nice."

Suddenly serious again, Clare ventured, "There's something more. You still think about Zoe, don't you?"

"Of course," Brett confessed, looking sideways at his partner. "I knew her for eleven days, you know. I try to convince myself that it was a short-lived privilege. But just eleven days!"

"You shouldn't torture yourself over her death."

"Her uncle shot her because she was mixing with me. It was my fault. I can't forget that. And tonight's fiasco reminded me that Zoe's uncle was another one that got away from me. I could have saved her if, in the heat of the moment, I hadn't fouled up my shooting."

Clare pulled up at a kerb, switched off the engine and turned to Brett sympathetically. "Here we are. I think you're going to need more than one beer. Come on. Let's go in."

As soon as she entered the house and took off her warm coat, Clare put on a cassette. "Music," she proclaimed. "It soothes the savage breast, or so someone once said."

"I think it takes more than music," Brett commented.

Over the meal, Clare said, "You know, we all have ones that got away. I certainly did. A week before my fourteenth birthday. My dad took me into town to buy a birthday present. A Sony Walkman, it was. They were new back then. Anyway, on the way home, we had to walk across a park. In a secluded part, we got mugged. At least, Dad did. At the time the mugger looked big and old to me. He was probably in his late teens. He pulled a knife on us. Dad refused to hand over his wallet and this chap went wild. Dad got cut up – seriously. The mugger ran off with my Walkman, still in its box. That's all he got. My dad was nearly killed for a cheap Walkman!" For a few seconds, Clare was silent. The background guitar music came to the fore until she spoke again. "I couldn't do anything. I was rooted to the spot. Afterwards, I felt really guilty. Dad had been knifed because of me, because it was my birthday present we'd gone out to get. And because I couldn't defend him. I guess it was a combination of shock, being scared stiff, and not knowing what to do. That's why I froze. So, you see, I let one get away. You're not the only one."

"I'm sorry, Clare," Brett said. "I didn't know. Now I understand why you have a thing about knives."

"Yes. I suppose that's where it comes from," she admitted. "Anyway, Dad's mugger wasn't the only one to get away. I've let plenty of crooks slip through my fingers. We all have. Sometimes, like today, it's because they outrun you. Sometimes, they stay right where they are, sitting pretty, and you know they're guilty as sin but you don't get the evidence. There's nothing you can do." She shrugged. "Failing to catch some of the baddies goes with the job."

"You're right, but..." Brett failed to finish his sentence. Instead he sighed and murmured, "It's a funny old game, as they say."

"What about our suspects for killing Games?" Clare prompted. "Simon's Mortimer's a new entry and Hannah Farr's still in the top ten?"

Brett nodded. "Just. She's not as high as Stephanie Games."

"Jordan only said Hannah wouldn't pull the

trigger. She might hold the gun for someone else – if it was pointed at a vivisectionist – and look the other way till the deed was done," Clare pronounced. "I'm still concerned about her."

"No scientific knowledge," Brett reminded his partner. "And no evidence she got heavy water from her father. But, you're right, we can't eliminate her yet. That's the problem. We do need to start narrowing it down soon. We need to disprove a few theories. We've got to trace the source of the heavy water."

"The nearest thing to finding a smoking gun," Clare observed.

"That's right," Brett agreed. "In the absence of a normal weapon, it's down to who had access to heavy water."

Clare added, "That's for the morning, yes? Right now, I want to finish my chilli in peace and relax."

"Yes. So do I," said Brett, confessing that he was enjoying her company.

Xenox was an oasis of lively business within an industrial desert. All around the drug company's large, bright and modern building were the sad, dilapidated and disused factories of Sheffield's steel industry. They were made more miserable by a shroud of dirty snow. Inside Xenox, security was just as tight as that at PHP. Once Clare and Brett had clearance, they were ushered into a coffee room where they were asked to wait for Paul Dunnett. Scientific magazines littered the low tables: *New Scientist*, *Laboratory News*, *Nature* and various pharmaceutical newsletters. Around the walls, there were shelves containing books on chemistry, biology, law and drugs.

When Dr Dunnett arrived and they were all settled into the easy chairs, Brett asked him, "What exactly is your position at Xenox?"

Paul sniffed and then answered, "Head of Analytical Chemistry." In his hand, he held a handkerchief at the ready. A streaming nose was the remnant of his cold.

"So you look after ... what? All the different instruments used to check the identity of potential new drugs?"

"Yes. And for analysing metabolites in humans and animals."

"Do your methods include NMR?" Brett enquired.

Paul seemed puzzled at the question but nodded. "Of course."

"So you're in charge of ordering the solvents you need for NMR – like heavy water?"

"Well," he replied, "I countersign the requisitions that my technician fills in."

"How much heavy water do you use?"

Dr Dunnett shrugged. "Quite a lot. It's a very useful solvent for our work with metabolites. Perhaps 100ml every week."

"And have you stepped up that amount recently?"

"Strange questions," Paul observed. He blew his nose noisily and then answered, "Not that I've noticed."

Brett asked, "Do you know what happens if you feed heavy water to a human?"

"No. But I could guess. If it's a small amount, next to nothing. If it's a lot, the body would go haywire, I imagine." With a frown on his face, Paul hesitated before murmuring, "Are you saying Colin Games's death was nothing to do with a drug for treating baldness after all? Was he murdered by administration of heavy water?" He seemed to be astounded.

"I didn't say any such thing," Brett responded, "but I am investigating a murder, not revising for a chemistry exam."

Paul exhaled loudly and sniffed twice. "Amazing. But I assure you I had no wish to see him dead and I certainly didn't have enough opportunity to poison him like that. It'd take time."

"Yet you *are* conspicuously aware of the effect of heavy water."

Dr Dunnett shrugged. "Any decent chemist would make the same educated guess. Ask yourself this. Would I have been so open if I'd murdered him with the stuff?"

Brett smiled. "I'd already asked myself that. And I'll keep the answer to myself. Before I leave," he added forcefully, "I need to see your orders for heavy water, say, in the past year."

Unruffled, Paul replied, "Fair enough. I haven't got anything to hide. Come to my office. I can call it up on the computer."

Brett and Clare left the premises with evidence of the steady use of heavy water by Paul Dunnett and his colleagues at Xenox. There had not been any apparent surges in the company's use of the water that was harmless in small doses but deadly in large quantities.

On the way to headquarters, Brett used his mobile phone to call the chemistry department of York University. The switchboard operator soon put him through to Dr Roger Bassindale. Brett introduced himself and informed the lecturer that he was gathering background information on Colin Games as part of an investigation into his death.

Dr Bassindale already knew that his ex-student had died in mysterious circumstances. "I heard from my friend, Derek Jacob," he explained. "He also told me – some time ago – that Colin had become a leading light at PHP. I was taken aback really."

"Why?" Brett queried.

"Because, to be honest, he wasn't my best student. He was solid enough, I suppose, but he lacked initiative. If he made a big success at PHP, I'd guess he stumbled upon something by good fortune rather than talent. Still, we all deserve some good luck in life." At the other end of the line, the chemist chuckled. "All his worthwhile work came from suggestions by another student and, as I recall, all his written work was copied from the same source. Now, what was his name? He went to Yorkshire Water but moved to Xenox."

Brett prompted, "It wouldn't be Paul Dunnett, by any chance?"

"Yes. That's it. Paul Dunnett. Now there was a bright kiddie. He heads his own section at Xenox now, I believe. Good for him. He deserves it. I always thought he'd make it big."

Concluding their brief but fascinating conversation, Brett said, “Thank you, Dr Bassindale. You’ve been very helpful.”

Suddenly, Brett was intrigued. He reported Roger Bassindale’s comments to Clare and added, “When we first interviewed Paul Dunnett he said Colin Games was a good chemist at university. Why would he say that if Games got all his best ideas from Dunnett himself?”

Clare frowned. “Strange.” She paused and then suggested, “Perhaps, if they were mates, he was just trying to be kind to his dead friend. When someone dies, we all remember the good bits and try to forget the shortcomings. We look at the dead through rose-tinted spectacles.”

“Perhaps,” Brett murmured. He was not convinced by Clare’s explanation.

Back in the police station, Liz updated them on her latest findings. So far, she hadn’t traced any scientists who had died with a miscellany of symptoms like Colin Games’s. “Oh. An E-mail’s just come in,” she said, clicking her mouse. “Apparently, Forensics has found seven distinct prints on the book. One belonged to Huxford, none matched with Loveday. Does that mean something to you?” After Brett nodded with a smile on his face, she went on to report that she’d discovered three companies that supplied heavy water. At first, none of them was willing to discuss their clients’ orders. Even so, Liz had persisted and discovered that, in the last few months, PHP had stepped up its use of heavy water.

"That's good work," Brett congratulated her. "Crucial. It puts PHP employees in the front line, and that includes Stephanie Games. In case she's disposing of her family one by one, we'd better look more carefully at Dean's health. Contact Tony Rudd and get the name of Colin Games's doctor. Dean's got the same doctor. Tony must have contacted the GP because he had a record of Colin Games's symptoms. I want you to go and see whoever it is. Try to find out if Dean's sickness really is the same as his dad's. OK?"

"Anything else?"

"Yes," Brett muttered. "It's only loosely connected with this case but it's important. Jordan Loveday – the one whose prints *weren't* on the book – he's at the university and he's a friend of one of our suspects—"

The telephone's ringing interrupted him. Liz answered the call and then put her hand over the mouthpiece. "It's a Mr Schulten for you, Brett. Want to take it?"

Brett smiled. "Sure do." He turned to Clare and said, "Why don't you fill Liz in about Jordan Loveday while I see what this is all about?"

Brett took the phone and said, "Hello, Mr Schulten. DI Lawless here."

"Good. I thought I'd better speak to you rather than fax some information on our use of heavy water. It's rather too delicate for fax transmission. You see, somewhat worryingly, it seems that in the past six months, our consumption of heavy water has increased alarmingly."

"I see," Brett replied, not revealing that he already had the same information from a different source. "Thanks for calling and letting me know." Eagerly, Brett continued, "Who ordered the extra amounts?"

"Well," Mr Schulten answered, "that's another embarrassing question. We thought the orders were signed by our NMR technician but she says she only filled in a fraction of them. Also, when you look closely, you can see the signature's slightly different from hers on most of the requisitions."

"Someone's forged them to get their hands on the heavy water," Brett deduced.

There was regret in Mr Schulten's voice. "That's what it looks like. I called you because I don't like the idea that someone has used my good company as a front for obtaining this substance."

"It has to be someone internal, as well," Brett inferred. "Your security wouldn't allow anyone to walk in and avail themselves of your solvents."

"No," Mr Schulten uttered in a resigned tone. "I have to agree with you. If I'm right in assuming that you believe Colin Games was poisoned with heavy water, it seems that I have his killer working for me."

Involuntarily, several names sprang to Brett's mind: Stephanie Games, Kelvin Raynor, Simon Mortimer and, of course, Mr Schulten himself.

"I guess," Mr Schulten was saying, "you'll want to visit us again."

"Certainly," Brett agreed. "From now on, my investigations will be centred on your company. First, I'd like to collect a few of those order slips. The forged ones and some of the legitimate ones for comparison. Then there's some examples of handwriting. I'll need handwritten documents by Stephanie Games, Simon Mortimer, Kelvin Raynor and yourself."

"Me?"

"Yes." Brett explained, "I have to be thorough and complete."

Mr Schulten sighed audibly. "Anything else?"

"I'll send in some forensic scientists to take water samples from Colin Games's office where he used to take breaks. I trust I have your full co-operation in all this?"

"I have little choice," Mr Schulten concluded gruffly.

Brett put down the phone and announced to Clare and Liz, "Bingo! We've got a good lead at last." He told them that the Managing Director of PHP had conceded that the murderer had almost certainly obtained the heavy water through his company.

"So," Liz presumed, "all efforts on PHP employees?"

"Nearly all," Brett answered. "In case we *have* got a domestic on our hands, see if you can get Forensics to speed up the analysis of water from the Games's house. But," Brett added in a low voice, "there's also this Jordan Loveday … unpleasantness. Put a bit of effort into that as well. When you can. If Huxford's our man – or someone else – either he's still got the books or they're in the hands of a dodgy dealer. Either way, let's dangle some bait and see if you get a nibble. We might land Huxford, a member of his staff or the dealer. Or Jordan Loveday, I suppose. A response from any of them would clear it up quickly. So, I think you play the part of a collector, Liz. You're after rare antique books. Put out an Internet call and newspaper ads saying you want to add a first edition of Isaac Newton's *Principia Mathematica* to your collection."

"Collect it? I can't even spell it!" Liz joked.

After picking up the order slips from PHP, Brett and Clare visited the graphologist yet again. While Brett shuffled the pieces of paper like a pack of cards and spread them out randomly in front of him, George was smiling merrily. Because of Brett's scepticism about his expertise, it amused and delighted him to play a central role in Brett's inquiry for the second time. He surveyed the slips for just a few seconds and then remarked, "Easy! No problem at all." Unerringly, he picked up and placed together all of the orders with genuine signatures and moved to one side all of the forgeries. When he'd finished, he looked up at Brett and asked, "Well? Does that put me in the superleague of geniuses?"

Brett nodded wryly. "How did you do it?"

"Two things," George proclaimed. He pointed to

the genuine slips and explained, "These signatures are authentic. See: they're smooth and continuous. The writer's started at the start of the surname and gone through to the end without lifting the pen from the paper. That's how we all write our signatures. Here," he continued, indicating the forgeries, "the signatures are quite good – the same size and shape as the authentic ones – but, to get it right, the forger's had to stop and start a lot. He – or she – has done it a letter at a time. See? They've done the 'l' here, concentrating on getting the loop right but then stopped. No doubt they were checking out how to do the next letter. You can see where they stopped the 'l' and started the 'a'. The progression isn't smooth from start to finish like the genuine article. Then there's the pen used. It's not my field really, but it's pretty obvious. The real signatures were done with a cheapo biro. It gives blobs of ink now and again like all cheap biros do. Probably one of those yellow and black pens – Universal Office Supplies, I should think. The forger's used an altogether classier biro. No ink blotches."

"Thanks," Brett said, acknowledging George's help. "Soon enough, I'll get the full works on the inks. I left a couple of slips with Trace Analysis so they can identify both inks. They're tackling it now – and over the weekend if necessary."

"No point checking for fingerprints?" George asked.

"By the time we got to these," he said, nodding

towards the order slips, "just about all our suspects had leafed through them, as well as half of the admin. department. I'd be more suspicious of someone whose prints *aren't* on them. It might mean they handled them with gloves." Brett looked more content than he had for days. It was because he could see a clear route to the finishing post. He thought that he was on the home straight. "No," he said happily. "Forget prints. Ink analysis will do the business. I got samples of handwritten reports from our main suspects at PHP. Traces will test them as well. If there's a match between a suspect's ink and the forged signatures, we find our heavy water hoarder. We find our culprit."

Feeling pleased with themselves, Brett, Clare and Liz retired to the club together in the evening. It was Friday and the place was packed with off-duty police officers. While Brett ordered the first round and his colleagues stood either side of him, a sergeant called Greg Lenton came towards them, crying, "Argh! It's the three witches!"

Brett nudged Liz and said, "Can't be referring to you. You couldn't spell."

Clare quoted, "'By the pricking of my thumbs, something wicked this way comes.'"

"You what?"

"One of the witches in *Macbeth*," Clare chirped.

"Great. That's all we need," Greg murmured good-naturedly. "A poet, a scientist and a techno-junkie. What's the police force coming to?"

"The formation of the dream team," Liz replied snappily.

Banter bounced across the room. Brett was pleased to be a part of it. When he'd first joined the squad, Greg had been particularly hostile towards him, most of the others had been antagonistic and only Clare had accepted him. Now, he was a member of a dream team. Amid the rowdiness, Brett said happily to Clare and Liz, "We've made good progress on this case. I think we can afford to give ourselves a weekend off."

"A weekend off?" Liz exclaimed. "What's that? I don't understand."

Clare took a draught of beer and then grinned. "It's when you get Saturday and Sunday to yourself, if I remember rightly. It means you get out the compass for some hill-walking, look the other way when you see someone pocket a video in Woolworths, get into the gym, watch Sheffield Wednesday get slaughtered. That sort of thing."

Liz shook her head. "A weekend off! Remind me to get assigned to you again some time, Brett. Obviously, you're not just a pretty face."

"However," he added, pausing dramatically, "if you want to volunteer to come in tomorrow, Liz, you can check if any results arrive by E-mail."

"Too late," she returned. "You already gave me the days off."

Clare looked at Brett and laughed.

"What's up with you?" Brett asked her.

"I can read you like a book," she admitted with a smile. "You've given us the weekend off but you'll be in to check the computer tomorrow, won't you? Too eager for those results."

Brett shrugged. "You must admit, we're so close to an answer, it's hard to walk away from it for a couple of days. Well, I find it hard. I'm too curious. Can't rest when there's still a mystery to solve."

Clare groaned histrionically. "What time?" she muttered. "I'll come in and keep you company."

"I need to do some shopping in the morning. I'm out of tropical fish food. How about after lunch? Say, two o'clock."

"It's a deal," Clare agreed.

In the city there was no new snow overnight. But it was just as cold. The soiled carpet of obstinate slush, ice and snow seemed set to be a permanent feature. Unlike the brilliant untrodden snow in the silent and serene Vale of Edale, it was grimy and unwelcome. Brett had heard on some documentary that Inuits had two hundred words for different types of snow. In Britain there was just one bland word for falling snow, snow that adhered to trees, deep snow, powdery snow. Such a small and singular word to describe the innumerable forms of the substance.

First thing in the morning, Brett pounded round the permafrost park and thought of water. There was an almost inconceivably large amount of it on the planet. He was running precariously on frozen water. The bushes grew white whiskers of water. His moist breath deposited watery droplets in the chilled air. Three-quarters of his body was water. A simple molecule but it gave life to everything. Where there was no water, there was no life. Yet a tiny, almost imperceptible, change to the water molecule led to death. Nature was astonishing and wonderful. It was also perverse and wilful.

Back at home, he showered before taking a long drink of fruit juice and eating his cereal. He placed the fallout from breakfast in the dishwasher and then pushed the maximum load of clothing into the washing machine. Passing his aquarium, he told his fish that they would have to wait for food until he had been to the garden centre. It seemed that his life was dominated by water.

At work, with Clare beside him, he gazed at the monitor. Disappointingly, the ink analyses had not yet been completed so the findings had not materialized in his computer. His folder did contain some new results, though. The samples of water from the Games house and PHP had been examined and the outcome E-mailed to Brett's terminal. Colin Games's office was devoid of dubious water but something had cropped up at his home. The house's tap water was normal but a jug of water, found right at the back of a kitchen cabinet, was mainly heavy water. The forensic scientist had taken the liberty of getting the container dusted. According to the report, there were three good fingerprints and a couple of partials on the jug. None of them belonged to Colin Games.

Straightaway, Clare picked up the telephone and called Forensics. "Clare Tilley and Brett Lawless," she said. "We need someone with a prints kit urgently. Operation Deep Water. Murder. Subjects: Stephanie and Dean Games." She dictated their address. "Cross-check them with the prints on..." She glanced at the report on the screen for the reference number of the water jug and continued, "Exhibit CG4. E-mail results to us as soon as possible, please. Thanks." She replaced the handset and remarked, "It's getting close to home, isn't it? I'd say we've got a straightforward domestic."

Brett nodded thoughtfully. "We know the culprit almost certainly works at PHP. Now, the murder weapon's turned up at the Games house. There's only one common factor, I must admit. Stephanie Games."

"She's got the scientific knowledge, the opportunity and a couple of motives. Money and freedom to chase her lover. Simon Mortimer even said she'd joined her husband for coffee breaks quite a bit recently. Taking another opportunity to poison him? I thought it was strange when he told us. It's not as if they were young lovers who couldn't bear to be apart. They're hardly the type to use any excuse to get together."

"Mmm. It all fits," Brett commented. "But..."

"But what?"

"I don't know," Brett murmured. "Just seems too easy. And no absolute proof." Brett's logical and creative mind had already begun to think of several convoluted possibilities.

"Well, I agree we haven't caught her with heavy water in her cupped hands," Clare uttered, "but the evidence is pretty good." She went on to remind him that the simplest theory was usually the best. "We need to bring in Stephanie Games, Brett."

"Let's hang on," Brett decided. "If the forged signatures were written with ink from her pen and if the prints on the water jug are hers, I'll be persuaded. Then we'd have a case against her."

"Watertight," Clare proclaimed with an ironic, satisfied smile.

Brett turned off the computer and asked, "What do you say to going and watching Wednesday's match? Even we deserve a bit of playtime."

"Nice idea," Clare replied. "Pity it was called off after the ref's inspection of the pitch this morning. Anyway," she added apologetically, "I arranged to go to the gym with some friends after this. Then I'm going to visit my mum and dad. I promised. They worry about me. Surrounded by villains. I have to show myself at least once a month so they can see I'm still in one piece."

"Oh. Never mind, then. Another time, maybe."

"Yeah," she said. "Another time."

Brett's schedules were too demanding and erratic to allow him to attend rugby training regularly enough to command a place in the South Yorkshire Police team. He was good enough, tough enough and fast enough, but his job prevented it. This weekend, with some time on his hands, he went along to the team's practice anyway and worked out with them. Brett's occasional appearances at training were welcomed by the club members because he was skilful but not competing for a place in the team. Afterwards, he felt bruised, tired and refreshed, and he had a few drinks in the bar with the rest of the players.

On Sunday, he experienced a strange impulse. Usually he only telephoned his parents when there was an occasion to mark. This time, he felt a need to call them without a particular reason. Like giving them a half-term report. As always, he had to check their number before dialling and, as always, he was apprehensive. It was his mother who answered. "Hello, Mum. It's Brett," he declared.

"Brett!" Her response fell midway between a question and an exclamation. "I didn't expect... How are you?" she asked tentatively.

"Fine. I just thought I'd call you," he said unnecessarily. He kicked himself for his ungainly nervousness.

"Is anything wrong?"

"No. It's fine. What's your weather like in Kent? Snowed in?"

"No," she answered. "Just a dusting of snow." She didn't enquire into the conditions in South Yorkshire.

Brett attempted to loosen her up with a different

approach. "How's Dad?" he asked.

"Oh, he's fine as well. Working hard, looking forward to early retirement. How's *your* job coming along?"

Persevering with the stilted and forced conversation, he replied, "It's good. That's why I'm calling, I suppose. I thought you might want to know I'm in charge of my first major inquiry. Bit of a landmark for me. A rather unusual murder." He paused, hoping that she'd show some curiosity or congratulate him. She did neither. "Anyway," he continued, "it's going well. Looks like an arrest tomorrow. I think the chief wants me to specialize in the bizarre cases. Thinks I've got a knack for them. Suits me."

Still there was no compliment. To discontinue the topic without being rude, she replied, "I suppose you can't tell me any more, it being police business."

He would have liked to share some of his thoughts, but he let her off the hook. "That's right. Top secret," he said, trying to inject a little humour. "I've got a partner. Name of Clare. She's great. We get on well."

"Did you get into any more trouble over that witness who died? What was her name?" Her tone was unfeeling, even harsh. She seemed faintly pleased to resurrect the topic and to imply blame all over again.

Reticently, Brett mumbled, "Zoe." In his Christmas call, he had told his parents only that she was a witness. He had kept to himself his deeper involvement with her.

"Got over it?" his mum asked curtly, more out of politeness than concern.

Brett's brain screamed, "No!" His mouth muttered, "Yes. It's over and done with."

"Well," his mum said. "It was good of you to phone."

Brett recognized that somewhere between himself and his mother, there was a very large brick wall. He was wrong to think that a telephone call might draw them together with a common interest in his career. "All the best to you both," he concluded and then he rang off.

He watched his aquarium for a while. The fish were equally incapable of showing fondness but at least they demanded attention, even if it was only for food and occasional fresh water. After a few minutes, he turned on the television and watched the local news. Courtesy of a quote from Detective Chief Superintendent Johnstone, Brett learnt that Sheffield chemist, Dr Colin Games, was the subject of a high-level murder investigation. Brett smiled wryly. "High level! A poet, a scientist and a techno-junkie. No expense spared."

On Monday, evidence arrived like snow in a blizzard. And all of it pointed in the same direction. The first report that was deposited in Brett's folder came from the fingerprint section. All of the prints on the water jug belonged to Stephanie Games's right hand. Next, Liz returned from her foray to Dean's surgery. "The doctor was only too happy to co-operate," she announced. "I felt like a priest he was keen to confess to. He was worried about Dean but he didn't want to come and talk to us about it because his dealings with his patient are confidential. But because I went to him, he felt justified in talking. No details, you understand. He was anxious not to compromise his position as keeper of his patient's secrets. So, all he would say is that Dean's symptoms are strikingly similar to the early ones shown by his father. The doctor didn't tell Dean himself for fear of frightening him."

"I can well imagine it would," Brett ventured. "But, when Dean spoke to us, he was already worried about that possibility. And Hannah had cottoned on to the connection as well."

"Now we know why Stephanie Games didn't dispose of the evidence," Clare put in. "She kept some heavy water at home because she's not finished her killing spree yet."

"I must admit," Brett said, "it's looking pretty damning."

The ink analysis confirmed it. The pen used by the NMR technician to sign the requisitions for heavy water contained a common ink easily identified by the International Ink Library. The ink from the forger's pen was unusual, not included in the library, but it matched precisely with some ink in an old report written by Stephanie Games.

"Shall I get a car?" asked Clare.

Brett nodded. "Yes. Let's pull her in." Turning to Liz, he said, "Better phone Dean's doctor and give him our best diagnosis. The early stages of poisoning by heavy water. According to articles on its biological effects, all Dean has to do is drink lots of proper water and flush it out. No lasting effect because it hasn't got to a critical level."

On the way to PHP, Clare said, "You're not happy about this case, are you? You're not convinced, even by a mountain of evidence."

"I should be," Brett replied. "Facts are facts, and there's no denying it looks clear-cut. But, no, I still don't feel confident. I suppose it's *because* of the mountain of evidence. She's an intelligent woman, Stephanie Games. I'm surprised she's left such a lot of incriminating clues in her wake."

"That's easy to explain," Clare voiced. "I should've thought of this before. Remember she never expected to be investigated. She used a devious method so that her husband's death would be put down to natural causes – so that murder would never be suspected. Under those circumstances, she wouldn't have to worry about leaving a trail because she didn't think anyone would be sniffing along it."

"OK. I take your point," Brett responded. "But it's too soon for her to start on her son as well. An intelligent woman would wait for the fuss to die down over her husband's death first."

"Maybe she's in a hurry. Desperate for the inheritance or for Michael Ashton."

The radio-phone announced the advent of more evidence. This time it concerned the stolen library books. Liz announced, "I got a bite on E-mail, from a Jordan Loveday."

"Oh. I hoped it wouldn't..." Brett was disappointed. He didn't want the case to be straightforward. He had sympathy for Jordan and didn't want him to be the villain. "Anyway, what was the message?"

"He's got a copy of *Principia Mathematica* for sale. Wants a cool £100,000 for it. What do you think?"

"Sounds a bit over the top to me. I'd pay £70,000 maximum."

"Very funny," Liz retorted. "With your salary you might, but not on a meagre Detective Sergeant's like mine."

"OK," Brett replied seriously. "Say you're interested but the price tag's rather heavy. Say you need to see the book to check its condition. Then, hopefully, he'll suggest a meeting. Lure him out into the open."

"Will do," she replied.

Brett added, "A question, Liz. Is it possible for someone else to send an E-mail using Jordan Loveday's name?"

"Sure is," Liz answered. "Just need to hack into Loveday's section of the computer and the infiltrator can send an E-mail under his identity. In the trade, it's called spoofing."

"Thanks, Liz," Brett said. "We should bear that in

mind. You may be talking to Loveday or … anyone." He signed off.

As soon as Brett announced to Stephanie Games that they wished to question her in connection with her husband's murder, she refused to say anything without her solicitor. They allowed her to call him from work so that by the time they'd whisked her back to the police station and placed her in an interview room, he was able to join her.

For the sake of the recording, Clare set up the interview formally, announcing who was present, when and where. Then Brett began. Keeping his doubts to himself, he said, "You already know your husband was killed, poisoned. By now, no doubt, you'll have heard the rumours that he was administered copious amounts of heavy water. How do you explain the fact that your pen was used to forge orders for heavy water at PHP?"

"Which pen?" she enquired abruptly.

"One you use at work. A biro. Probably an uncommon one."

"Ah," she replied. "This one." She rummaged in her handbag and then extracted her gold-plated biro. "It was a present from Colin. Some time ago he went to a conference in Budapest. He brought it back for me. It disappeared a couple of months ago. I lost it. I only found it again recently."

"Where did you lose it?"

"I'm not sure. I thought I put it in my bag but I

couldn't find it when I got to work one day. It turned up where all biros turn up eventually: between the cushions of the sofa. I must have missed when I went to put it in my handbag and it fell into the crack without me noticing."

"What's the name of PHP's NMR technician?" asked Brett.

"I've no idea," she answered. "I don't have anything to do with that section."

Interjecting, her lawyer grunted, "I hope you've got something more substantial than a pen, Inspector Lawless. My client's biro may be distinctive, but it doesn't prove anything. Besides, anyone could have used it, as Dr Games has just suggested."

"OK." Brett turned to Stephanie and asked, "How about the jug of heavy water in your house, with your fingerprints all over it?"

"I don't know." Her expression suggested trepidation. She realized that she'd been presented with some hard evidence and seemed to be at a loss to explain it. "If I'd poisoned Colin – and I assure you I didn't – I would've got rid of the excess."

"Not if you had further use for it," Brett observed. "Your son has the beginnings of the same symptoms as your husband."

"You can't be serious! I wouldn't..." She ran out of words to express her indignation. "That's ridiculous," she gasped.

"It did have your fingerprints on it," Brett stressed.

Her lawyer put in, "Anyone could have planted the water in a jug that Dr Games used frequently."

Ignoring him, Brett continued to apply pressure. "You've got the necessary chemical knowledge and you had plenty of opportunity to poison your husband over a considerable time period. Dean told us that Colin always expected you to do the housework, shopping and cook – despite your job."

For an instant, Stephanie looked startled and her mouth opened but she changed her mind about saying something and remained silent.

"Did you take breaks at PHP with your husband?"

"No. Too busy," she answered.

"We have information that you did."

"Then your information's wrong," she growled.

"Tell us about your relationship with Michael Ashton."

"What's he got to do with it?" she snapped. Then, realizing that Brett was probing her motives, she answered, "Not much of a relationship. Just a passing affair. A brief flirtation. I said my husband wasn't easy to live with."

Clare asked, "When did you last see Michael Ashton?"

"Some time ago," she replied.

"A week? Two weeks? A month?" Clare persisted.

"I saw him at New Year," she admitted.

"So," Brett surmised, "this affair wasn't as brief as you implied. I suggest it's more like infatuation."

"No," Stephanie barked. "He's a little creep,

really. I know that. But, well, we all need a little attention sometimes. He's there when I want some attention."

Brett smiled wryly. He remembered that Ashton had said something similar. His reaction was that, if all else failed, Stephanie was available. Perhaps the two of them deserved each other, Brett thought, but their relationship did not seem to be worth the drastic risk of committing murder. "Do you have any money problems?" Brett enquired. "And remember, we'll check."

Stephanie shook her head. "I think the appropriate word is comfortable. I had no need to kill Colin for his money. I don't gamble or fritter cash on drink or drugs or whatever. I like the odd exotic holiday but Colin never denied me that. Besides, my own salary wasn't far short of his till PHP started to shower him with bonuses. I don't spend more than my own income."

"Inspector Lawless," the lawyer uttered, feigning impatience, "you're not convincing either me or my client that you have a case against her. And you have certainly not established a motive of any sort."

"Let's be honest," Brett said to Stephanie. "Either you're guilty or," he proposed adamantly, "you're protecting someone."

"That's not a question," her lawyer intervened. "You don't have to respond."

Taking his advice, Stephanie bowed her head and remained silent.

"Are you going to charge my client?" the solicitor snorted.

Brett stood up. "To be decided," he announced brusquely. "The inquiry continues. Interview concluded at eleven forty-five." He looked at Clare and commented, "We need to talk."

Clare followed Brett out of the room.

"What do you think?" Brett asked her.

Clare shrugged. "Good liar or pure as the driven snow," she responded with a groan.

"And if I pushed you off the fence, which side would you fall?"

"Whichever way you pushed me," she answered evasively.

"OK. It's too close to call. Let's think about the facts." Brett leant against a wall and sighed. "What we've got so far doesn't add up to a strong case. I know the done thing is to believe the simplest theory until facts refute it. I know none of our facts do refute it. More than that, they all suggest she's guilty. But I still can't believe the simplest theory. There's something not quite right about it. You know," he added, "if this was science, we'd still believe the simplest theory – supported by the facts – but only because we hadn't done the right experiments to get the contradictory evidence." Brightening, Brett said mysteriously, "That's it, of course. Extra experiments. Extra data. We haven't asked all the right questions yet."

He flew back into the interview room and resumed the interrogation. "Did you go into work with your husband, Dr Games, and go home with him?" Brett asked her.

Stephanie looked puzzled but answered, "Yes. In the car."

"And what did you carry with you? A briefcase?"

"No. Security doesn't allow us to take work home. I take a handbag or nothing at all."

"I see."

"What's this about?" Stephanie queried.

"Contrary to what you – and your lawyer – might think, I'm trying to find facts that prove your innocence. The illegal orders for heavy water were for large volumes. Big, heavy bottles. Not ideally suited to a small handbag. Some might suggest that you'd find it difficult to smuggle such containers out of PHP, right under your husband's nose."

On hearing Brett's remark, Stephanie did not display any relief. She continued to look glum.

Brett pushed towards her two pieces of paper. "Here's another opportunity to prove your innocence."

Clare butted in, "Detective Inspector Lawless has

given the suspect Exhibit CG5 – a signed order slip for heavy water – and a blank piece of paper."

Brett continued, "I want you to copy that signature with your biro."

"Why?"

"Because someone did. Someone used your pen to forge that signature and get the heavy water. That's for sure. If it wasn't you, you won't mind trying to copy the name so I can show it to our graphologist. He'll soon be able to tell whether your attempt matches the forgeries that we have." Actually, Brett did not know if the task was within George's repertoire, but it was either true or an effective bluff.

Stephanie hesitated. She asked her solicitor, "Do I have to do this?"

"Of course not," he replied, dismissing Brett's approach. "But…"

Interceding, Brett agreed, "Of course you don't. But it *is* a golden opportunity to give me a solid fact that disproves the theory that you killed your husband. It would eliminate you straightaway. Why should you refuse?"

Stephanie put her head in her hands and groaned almost inaudibly.

"I'll tell you why you're refusing. As I said before, either you're guilty or you're protecting someone. Who, Stephanie? Why won't you write on a piece of paper to show you didn't forge those heavy-water orders?"

She was sobbing quietly to herself, still covering

her face with trembling hands.

"I'd like to request a little time with my client," her lawyer chipped in. "As you can see, she's in some distress."

"All right," Brett said. "But, first, let me say this. I don't believe an intelligent person would leave so many incriminating pointers. I don't believe you'd risk taking home the heavy water with your husband – even if you could get the large bottles in your handbag – which I doubt. It would be like showing him a loaded shotgun. And I don't believe you're refusing to copy a signature because you're guilty. If you were, you'd probably have a bit more bravado. Knowing how you'd written the technician's name before, you'd try to write it differently this time, and fool our graphologist. That wouldn't be too tricky. But you didn't go for it. You refused to write *because* it'd prove your innocence!" Brett paused and exhaled. "I'm sorry, Stephanie, but I can't offer him any protection. I have to go and get him." Brett walked out, saying to her solicitor. "I'm not releasing her yet but for now she's yours. You'd better have a serious talk with your client, and explain the repercussions of obstructing my inquiries."

In the office, Clare peered at her partner and said, "If she's innocent, you've got to ask yourself who framed her good and proper."

"I've already done that," Brett responded.

"I guess we both have," she murmured, "and I guess we both know. So does Stephanie."

"Yes. It's just dawned on her who killed her husband. Who could have easily removed that biro from her bag and slipped it down the sofa later? Who could easily pour heavy water into a jug that was certain to bear her prints? Who else had ample opportunity to poison Colin Games? Who's the only person she'd feel she had to protect?"

"But how would Dean get hold of the heavy water?" Clare queried. "And he doesn't have the scientific knowledge," she asserted.

"Exactly. Someone at PHP's behind him. The person he gave the pen to – and who returned it afterwards. The person who smuggled out the heavy water and gave it – with instructions – to Dean. Let's go and find out."

"How?"

Brett shrugged. "It'll take ten minutes to drive there. That's ten minutes to decide tactics. Should be enough." Brett hesitated and then added, "Let's pick up a couple of sandwiches on the way."

In the car, Brett radioed Liz and asked her to go to the sixth-form college, arrest Dean Games on suspicion of the murder of his father and take him into custody. "Get yourself some uniformed assistance. Then let him sweat in a cell till we get back. No contact with his mother yet," Brett requested.

As she drove towards PHP, Clare mentioned Dean's illness. "What do you make of *that*? If he's our culprit, it's strange he's being poisoned as well."

"A bold attempt to throw us off the scent and

frame his mother," Brett proposed. "He must be drinking heavy water himself. All part of the plan with his accomplice. I bet Dean's in good hands. This chemist, whoever it is, has probably worked out a diet of heavy water that just makes Dean slightly unwell. Remember, there's no lasting effect unless it gets to a critical level. Not a huge risk. A penalty well worth paying to avoid prosecution for murder."

"OK," Clare said, "but *why* did he take part in his dad's murder?"

"Not sure till we talk to him. Maybe Hannah Farr persuaded him to do it as an animal-rights protest. Or maybe she seduced him into acting as her benefactor. He needs the inheritance to fund his girlfriend."

After parking the car outside the drug company, Clare opened the driver's door. Before she could leave, Brett said, "Hang on. Let's just stay here for a bit. It's lunchtime!"

Puzzled, Clare closed the door again. She turned to face her partner.

Brett got out his mobile phone and said, "First, I'm going to phone Mr Schulten. See what havoc we can create inside."

"You'll be lucky," she replied. "Bet you only get his secretary."

Brett smiled. "That's what I'm banking on." He called the company and asked for the Managing Director. As Clare had predicted, he was put through to a secretary.

"He's in a meeting, I'm afraid," she reported efficiently. "Would you like to leave a message?"

"Yes. A very important and urgent one." Brett explained that he was the detective in charge of the inquiry into Colin Games's death. "I'm on my way to see you and I'm anxious to talk to Mr Schulten, Kelvin Raynor and Simon Mortimer as soon as I arrive," he told her. "So, to make sure they're free to see me, please give this message to all of them. If Mr Schulten's meeting's still in progress, I'm sure he'd want to be slipped a note. We've just arrested Dean Games for the murder of his father. Dean's told us he has an accomplice at PHP. We're on our way. We'll arrive in fifteen minutes. Have you got that?"

"Yes," the secretary replied, clearly disconcerted by the message. She read it back to Brett so that he could check its accuracy.

"That's it," Brett confirmed. "You'll appreciate that it must be delivered immediately to Kelvin, Simon and Mr Schulten."

"Of course," she said dutifully. "I'll do it as soon as I put the phone down."

"Thank you," Brett replied. He put away the phone and smiled at Clare. "Now we just wait and see what develops," he declared. "We've prodded. Let's see who squeals."

"Hope it's more a case of firing the starting pistol and seeing who runs."

"Fancy a chase, do you? Got your spikes on?" Brett chuckled. Behind the banter, he felt anxious and determined. There was no guarantee that his scheme would succeed. There was no guarantee that he'd just frightened the accomplice so much that he'd attempt to make a dash for it before the police arrived.

Chewing on their sandwiches, they settled down to wait.

Eight minutes later, a very tall employee scurried out of the security building and headed for the car park.

Clare looked at Brett and her eyebrows rose. "Our honest Yorkshireman. Well, well. Want to follow him by car?" she asked. "See where he runs to?"

"I'd love to, but it's too big a risk if we lose him. This one's not going to get away from me. Drive round to the entrance and block him in."

Clare turned on the ignition and put her foot down. Racing to the gate was the nearest she'd ever got to a car chase. She almost felt deprived, upstaged by her television counterparts. Stopping the unmarked car right across the lane, she got out, wiped the baguette crumbs from her coat and leant on the roof. On the passenger's side, Brett did the same.

Simon's face, viewed through the windscreen of the approaching car, first displayed anxiety. When he was close enough to realize who was blocking his escape, panic set in. At that point, Clare thought he was going to accelerate and ram them. But a second later, he decelerated with resignation in his expression. He stopped the car and hung his head.

Brett walked to his door and opened it. Inside, Simon looked like a huge crouching insect snared inside a tiny cage. "Leave your car here," Brett ordered. "We're taking you in for questioning regarding the murder of Dr Colin Games."

Simon sighed wearily and then thumped his steering wheel with both hands. "I'm saying nothing," he mumbled dismally.

Brett kept his suspects well away from each other, installed in three separate interview rooms. "Where do we start?" he asked himself.

Clare grinned at him. "Spoilt for choice."

Before Brett decided, Liz arrived to complicate matters. "Things are still moving fast. You had a call from the library. Apparently, Loveday has been booted out of the university, subject to an appeal. And I had an E-mail. Loveday wants to meet me tonight, to discuss the deal with that book."

"Tonight!"

"Never a dull moment," Clare pronounced.

Brett shook his head. "I could do without the distraction tonight."

"Sorry," Liz responded. "But he didn't give me a choice. Said he'd got a dealer interested in it so if I wanted it, I'd have to move quick."

Brett sighed. "OK. When and where?"

"The Maltings Restaurant in the city centre. Eight o'clock. I'm to give my name to the desk, presumably so Jordan can ask who I am when he comes in, and join me."

Trying to keep their spirits up, Clare put in, "Perhaps he'll buy you a meal."

"All right," Brett said. "You get there early. Check on the restaurant's exits. Try to persuade the powers-that-be to give you enough back-up to cover all doors and fire exits. Get a car in position right outside the entrance. We'll take up residence in it just before zero hour. Reserve yourself a table in the window so we can see you from the car. We'll move in as soon as he sits down with you and produces the book. No action till we see the goods. We need to catch him red-handed, so there's no doubt. I want to wrap it up tonight. So," Brett concluded, "you'd better do some research on the restaurant and the book this afternoon. That's your job while we have words with Dean and Simon Mortimer."

"Mathematical Principles of Natural Philosophy – or *Principia*, as it's universally known," Liz said with the proud smile of a student who has completed her homework early. "Sir Isaac Newton, 1687. The greatest science book every written. He managed to quantify the laws of motion, orbital mechanics and gravity, from Saturn's satellites to pendulums swinging on Earth, in a framework of an infinite three-dimensional space and absolute time. He used a mathematical model with a precision that amazed his contemporaries. Or so says my CD-ROM encyclopaedia."

Brett laughed and congratulated her. "I'm impressed. Ten out of ten. It should see you through the first exchanges with our book thief. Persuade him that you're serious, and persuade him to produce the goods. This afternoon you can concentrate on securing the area around The Maltings." As Liz walked away, Brett turned to Clare and asked, "Dean first? Probably easier to crack?"

"Probably," Clare agreed.

"Here's the catch," Brett announced. "I want you to take the lead. You're good with his age group. More experienced than me."

"Usually with arson, joy-riding or thieving."

"Time for promotion to the Premier League," said Brett.

After the formalities, Clare asked the young man, "You know why you're here, don't you, Dean?"

"Yes and no," Dean replied, grumbling. "I know you're trying to find out who murdered Dad, but I don't know what it's got to do with me."

"Who told you it was definitely murder?"

"Mum said you'd told her."

Clare nodded. "And how was he murdered?"

"How should I know?" Dean blurted.

"Oh, that's right," Clare muttered. "It's got nothing to do with you, has it?"

"No." Dean looked into the expressionless faces of both police officers but they didn't say anything so he continued, "I know I'm ill. I know I'm being poisoned as well." Exasperated, he added, "I told you before who's behind it."

"You were keen to tell us about your mum's lover, keen to imply she was after your dad's money. Keen to blame her," Clare remarked. "Why? What's your evidence?"

"Because..." Unsure of himself, he hesitated.

"Why?" Clare repeated. She suspected that he'd realized he was in danger of incriminating himself if he told her too much. He could not mention the jug of heavy water and the disappearing biro because an innocent bystander would not know about those things.

"Well, I don't have any hard evidence. You know that from the last time we talked. It's just a feeling, I suppose, but I know. I live with her so I know."

"To the best of your knowledge, has she been in touch with Ashton since your dad died?"

"She wouldn't, would she? She's cautious. She'd wait a while."

"Has she been out on spending sprees?"

"Same again," Dean answered. "She's waiting a respectable time before she does anything like that."

"Yes. That makes perfectly good sense," Clare

murmured amicably. "It means, though, that we can't see for ourselves any evidence for these motives you're suggesting."

Dean shrugged. "Suppose not," he croaked.

"Any cautious killer would wait a while – till she's in the clear – before reaping any benefit or taking any action. That's what you're saying."

"Yes," Dean said with impatience.

"So why's she poisoning you now, do you think?"

"What?"

"Isn't it a bit early to try the same trick on you? Wouldn't she wait a respectable time before she does anything like that?"

"I … er … I don't know," he mumbled angrily.

Clare smiled pleasantly at him. "I'm only quoting you, Dean."

"Perhaps she's in a hurry to get her hands on *all* of the money," he stammered. "Perhaps she's planning to get the lot before she splashes out."

"Mmm. Maybe. But it's all getting a bit messy now, isn't it? Not so clear-cut. She's waiting for some things but cracking on with others. Not very consistent."

Dean was at a loss for words. He just shrugged again.

"Still, I suppose that's life," Clare muttered. "Always more complicated than we'd like it to be. How about Simon Mortimer? Know him?"

Dean seemed shocked for an instant. "I've heard of him. Heard Dad mention him at home."

"Oh!" Clare uttered, feigning surprise. "We've had a chat with him and he claims you've met. Claims he knows you quite well. Are you saying he's wrong?"

Dean's blank expression remained fixed as a means of keeping panic away. "No. We did..." He lapsed into confused silence.

"How did the two of you get together?" Clare asked, while Brett watched the proceedings.

"The two of us?" Dean's head drooped. He was trying desperately to get his confused thoughts in order. Eventually he looked up and murmured, "He's the very tall chap, I think. If I'm right, we met at a PHP social. I got dragged along by Mum and Dad."

"And what did you talk about?"

"Can't remember. It was a long time ago."

"Did you discuss a plot to murder your father?" asked Clare firmly.

Dean collapsed on to the desk, putting his head in his hands.

"Well?" Brett put in.

Dean looked up and stared at them wildly. "I just don't know why you're accusing me! Why don't you go and get Mum?"

"Because she didn't do it, Dean," Clare replied in a quiet, sympathetic tone. "I think we all know who did." She glanced at Brett and said, "We're going to leave you here for a while to think about it. We'll be back." As she stood up, she added, "It's not wise to protect other people, Dean. You can end up carrying the can on your own."

In the corridor, Brett looked at his watch. "We're OK for time. Let's have a coffee," he proposed, "and then kick off with Mortimer. Dean can stew for a bit." As they strolled towards the coffee machine, Brett said, "Dean reacted oddly when you asked about the *two* of them, Dean and Simon, getting together."

"Yeah. I noticed," Clare replied, pushing the button for black coffee, no sugar. "Do you think there were more conspirators? Three, four?"

"I don't know," Brett answered. "But I'm sure you were right at the end. First, his mum tries to protect *him* – presumably because he's her son. Now *he's* protecting someone else. Why?"

"Who? I don't see why he wouldn't shop Mortimer. So, I don't think it's him. Perhaps it's the mysterious third man he's protecting."

They didn't bother to sit down to drink their coffees. It was only a few minutes before they were striding eagerly back towards the suite of interview rooms.

Colin Games's lanky technician had requested the presence of a solicitor and, to Brett's and Clare's first questions, he responded, "I have nothing to say."

Brett smiled and remarked, "Silence won't help you a great deal, Simon. We've already squeezed a lot of the juice out of young Dean Games. In a nutshell, he supplied you with his mum's biro, you supplied him with heavy water. He made lots of drinks for his dad. Maybe you did at work as well but we can't prove that yet."

"I have nothing to say."

"You lied about Stephanie Games gatecrashing your tea and coffee breaks at work to be with her husband. You said it to cast doubt on her. All part of the frame-up."

Simon stared silently at the detectives.

"You co-operated in the scheme to kill Colin Games – maybe you initiated it – because you hated him. You wanted to get your own back for all that maltreatment in the lab. You wanted to be rid of a bad boss."

"I told you I didn't like him," Simon snarled. "You know that. Doesn't mean I'd kill him."

"Perhaps you didn't – directly. You're an accessory to murder, though."

"You've got no proof of that."

"Why did you run from PHP, then? Because you're innocent? I doubt it. And why does Dean say what he says if you didn't give him the idea, the heavy water, and tell him how to use it?"

Simon frowned. "I didn't," he snapped.

"Didn't what?"

"Didn't give him the idea and I didn't tell him how to use it."

"So," Brett inferred, "you're not denying supplying heavy water."

The lawyer cut in, saying, "Mr Mortimer hasn't admitted any such thing. And it seems you have no proof that he did. Only the word of a spiteful boy, eager to place the blame elsewhere, no doubt."

"You'd know all about heavy water," Brett baited Simon. "Didn't you say you'd worked for a while in the water industry?"

"Yes. Yorkshire Water. But, in case you didn't know, they only deal with normal drinking and river water."

Brett stood up. "Very interesting. Before I go, tell me where you met Dean Games. We know you know him."

"He … er … came to a PHP social once."

"We'll resume this little discussion later tonight or tomorrow morning." Trying to draw a reaction from him, Brett said, "I've already cluttered our cells with another two suspects. You can be the third."

"Third?" Simon exclaimed.

"I'm going for a full house," Brett said.

Clare went to fetch the key for Liz's car and to find out its registration number while Brett went to speak to Stephanie Games. "You can go," he informed her, "if you can give me the answer to a question. Has Dean ever been to a social event at PHP?"

Concerned about her son, she cried, "Why? Why are you asking about Dean?"

Brett had to ignore her anguish. "It's a simple enough question," he stated. "Has he been to a social event at PHP?"

Stephanie frowned and shook her head. "No. I don't think so."

"Certain?"

She paused for thought and then answered, "Yes."

"OK. Thanks. I'll tell the custody officer to sort you out. Dean's here, though, and he'll have to stay with us. We've already charged him with murder."

When Stephanie began to shake and weep, all that Brett could do was murmur, "I'm sorry." He disliked trampling over people to get to the truth and delivering bad news but both were inescapable parts of the job.

Afterwards, Brett told Clare that his brief exchange with Stephanie had verified that the PHP social was a fabrication.

"So," his partner observed, "they'd taken the trouble to come up with the same story about their meeting. The same lie."

"Yes," Brett murmured thoughtfully. "Or they hit it lucky. Either way, they didn't meet at a party. The link between them's still a mystery. But..."

Clare looked at him expectantly.

He sighed heavily. "I don't know. There could be a convoluted connection between Mortimer and Dean Games. I need to speak to Mr Schulten." Picking up a phone, he dialled PHP and persevered until he got the Managing Director himself on the line. "Just one quick but very important question," Brett said. "I gather it's common practice for companies like PHP to infiltrate organizations like the Campaign for

Animal Rights. Did you ever send Simon Mortimer to CAR meetings?"

"No. We used to have someone on the inside but it wasn't Simon Mortimer. It was someone from our Luton outpost."

Disappointed, Brett said, "OK. Thanks anyway."

"No joy?" Clare enquired.

"Not yet," Brett replied. He had not given up, though. Calling the Control Room, he requested the name and number of the Managing Director of Xenox. Ten minutes later, he got the information that he wanted. The Head of Xenox was a Dr Roberts, and his secretary had informed Control that he was working at home. Immediately, Brett called Dr Roberts's home number, introduced himself and asked whether the pharmaceutical company had a faithful employee reporting from within the Campaign for Animal Rights.

The Managing Director refused to answer over the telephone. "Let's face it," he argued, "you could be anyone. You say you're a detective but you could be a CAR activist."

"All right," Brett responded. "I understand your qualms. But in that case I'd like to come to you right now. I can show you my ID and get the answer. It's vitally important to a major murder inquiry."

Dr Roberts did not sound enthusiastic. "I'll agree to give you my address if I can call South Yorkshire Police first and check your credentials with them. Detective Inspector Lawless, you say. I apologize if you're above board but, if you are, you'll appreciate my reticence. Organizations like CAR can be devious and … troublesome."

"That'll be fine," Brett answered. "I understand your vigilance. I'll expect you to call back shortly." He dictated his number to Dr Roberts.

After a few minutes, Dr Roberts phoned, saying, "Everything seems to be in order so you may make a short visit." He told Brett where he lived.

Immediately, Brett said to Clare, "To Totley, driver!"

"Yes, sir!" Clare boomed as they headed for a car.

At first, Brett thought that it was going to be a wasted trip. Dr Roberts denied that Xenox had anyone on the inside of any animal-rights group. "However," he added, "we *did* have someone a little while ago."

"When?"

"He stopped going some weeks ago. It got too dangerous for him because he thought that a CAR member had an inkling of who he really was."

"And who was he?"

"Paul Dunnett. For a while, he kept an ear to the ground for us."

With a giant smile, Brett said, "Thank you, Dr Roberts. That's what I needed to know."

Brett and Clare left Dr Roberts with all of his own questions unanswered.

Getting Clare to drive to Paul Dunnett's house, Brett announced, "If Dunnett was a Xenox mole, there *is* a link between Simon Mortimer and Dean Games. It's even more roundabout than I thought."

"What is it, then?"

"Yorkshire Water might be the key," Brett suggested. "On the phone, Paul Dunnett's old tutor, Roger Bassindale, said Dunnett worked there before he moved to Xenox."

"And Simon Mortimer was there as well," Clare interjected, recalling the interview with him earlier. "Their paths might have crossed. They might have been quite close once," she deduced. "So much for simple theories. There could be a third man – and a fourth woman!"

"Yes," Brett agreed. "Mortimer's got a motive and maybe he knows Dunnett. Dunnett – I don't know his motives – but he could've met Hannah Farr at a gathering of the CAR clan. And Hannah leads to Dean. That's the link. Or," Brett added as a word of caution, "is it all just too elaborate? Am I coming up with a fancy theory when there's a much simpler one staring at us?" He was worried that his imagination had again embroidered the facts too intricately.

"Here we are," Clare said, stopping the car. "We'll ask Dunnett if it's all too complicated."

This trip *was* a waste of time. The cold-ridden chemist was not at home. No one answered the door chimes, the lights were out and there were no sneezes from inside to give him away.

"Never mind," Brett said as they went back to the parked car. "We know where he'll be in the morning.

We'll talk to him at Xenox, first thing. Right now, let's go back and see if we can loosen Dean up a bit. We've just got time before our date at The Maltings. I want to know who's the choirmaster of our duo, trio, quartet or whatever it is."

"If you're right, I understand Dean's impression of a clam," Clare noted. "If Hannah's in on it, by not telling us anything, he's protecting her. Now, we tell him we know she's involved and he might just open up."

"There's something I still don't understand, though," Brett admitted. "Roger Bassindale said Colin Games was pretty poor, intellectually. Paul Dunnett said he was bright. Both of them can't be right. One of them's lying or has a dodgy memory."

Dean Games was hauled up from a cell and back into an interview room. He looked wretched but not yet broken.

Clare surveyed him and said, "Not very nice, are they, our cells? But..." She shrugged. "You'll have to put up with it till we sort out your involvement in your dad's death."

"Have you arrested Mum yet?" he asked.

"No, Dean," Clare replied, quietly. "You know – and we know – she was set up to take the blame. You've got to let go of that idea so we can begin to make progress. You took heavy water from Simon Mortimer and made sure your dad drank it. That's what really happened, isn't it?"

Dean grimaced bitterly. "No!"

"We don't blame you, Dean. You can admit it

because we don't think you're the main culprit here. We think you were manipulated, taken advantage of, by others. Someone else made you do it." Clare looked into Dean's face and continued, "Simon gave you enough of this special water to take yourself, just enough to make you ill, making your mum look guilty. And enough to plant in your mum's jug. So, you see, Simon's already spilled the beans. There's not much point carrying on with this story about your mum."

"He's lying!" Dean yelled.

"Let's try this," Clare said. "We also know who else is involved. It's not just you and Mortimer. We know Simon got you the murder weapon but how did he persuade you to use it on your dad? He didn't, did he? Someone else did that. Someone you must be very fond of."

Dean stared at her, aghast. His horrified expression told Brett and Clare that they had hit a raw nerve but he still refused to speak.

"Hannah was killing three birds with one stone, if you'll forgive the expression. She was protesting about PHP's use of animals by killing your dad and, on top of that, getting your mum locked away for it. Then she would have benefited again from the money you were set to inherit."

Dean's head dropped for a moment, then he peered at Clare and bawled, "Have you got Hannah here? Have you spoken to her?"

"We're talking to you, Simon and a number of

others," Clare answered calmly. "The fact is, we know about Hannah. Now, we'd like you to tell us your version of how you got in touch with Simon Mortimer. Not at some social, but through Hannah."

"Did Mortimer say?"

"No," Clare replied. "That's why we're asking you. We know about Simon Mortimer, yourself and Hannah. That's all. If there was someone else, he's going to get away with it unless you say something. You can't shield Hannah any more, Dean, so you might as well come clean. We need to know who masterminded this whole thing."

Dean groaned and sobbed for some time. Neither Clare nor Brett intervened as the young man disintegrated. They both felt for him but they had a job to do. His suffering would only be ended after a confession, penitence and punishment.

"All right," he said in a choking voice. "I'll tell you. There *was* someone else. He was the one who set it all up. First, we were just going to make Dad ill. That's what he said, anyway. He'd worked out exactly how much of the water we'd need. But then he said we'd all be better off if Dad was dead. Said we should carry on. Keep going with this poisonous water stuff. He worked out how we could pass the blame. He said everything would be OK." The words of explanation began to tumble from him rapidly and chaotically, like a river in flood. "Simon would be rid of his boss. CAR could boast it had executed one vivisectionist and jailed another. That's what he said.

And then there was me. You know, Dad always went on at me for not doing something worthwhile with my life. He reckoned science was the only way forward. Always made fun of me and my painting. Said design was just packaging. Not suitable for his son. Science and computing were the only things worth doing these days." Dean sniffed and wiped the moisture from his mouth and nose. "But it wasn't just that. There's Hannah as well. She needed money. She was in trouble herself and trying to fund quite a bit of CAR's operation. I gave her all I could but it wasn't enough. She'd have left me, you know, without... But I wasn't going to be without much longer. An inheritance on the way. She wouldn't leave me if I was rich. With Dad gone and Mum away, I'd have kept her."

Clare wanted to reach across the table and comfort him, but she let him be. She was saddened by the notion of a relationship that was gelled only by cash. She doubted that Hannah felt anything for Dean. It was likely that she was just using him to get at his parents and their money.

"Dean," Clare said, "I know it's not easy but it'll be better when you've told us everything."

Interrupting her, Dean snarled, "That's what *he* said! We'd all be better."

"Who was he, Dean? What's his name?"

Dean drew his hand across his dribbling mouth again. "Phil Arnold."

"Phil Arnold?"

"Yes."

Clare and Brett looked at each other with the same question written on their faces. *Who on earth is Phil Arnold?*

Clare tried not to appear shaken and confused by his revelation. "And how did Phil benefit from your father's death?" she enquired. "How did he say he'd be better off?"

"He didn't. I wasn't interested in his reasons. Only mine and Hannah's."

Still hiding her shell-shock, Clare tried a different approach. "Where does he come from? Where does he live or work? Do you know?"

"No idea," Dean mumbled. "He didn't say much apart from organizing … you know."

Outside the interview room, Brett looked at his watch. "It's getting late," he remarked. "But we can't leave it like that. Not with a name we've never heard of. There's one quick thing we can do before we head for the restaurant."

They rushed to Interview Room Three. Unhelpfully, Simon Mortimer swore that he'd never heard of Phil Arnold. Simon's lawyer advised against his answering any further questions so they hurried away.

Clare still clung to her opinion of the technician. As she drove towards the city centre, she ventured, "Maybe Mortimer isn't telling us everything, but I'm sure most of what he *has* said is true. He's still a down-to-earth Yorkshireman. He hasn't got a clue about Phil Arnold."

"Neither have I," Brett mumbled in frustration.

Clare parked the car in the only available slot – illegally, on double-yellow lines. Switching to Liz's car, they tried to focus for a while on a different case. From her car, they could see Liz in profile as she sat at a table, waiting for her dinner guest.

"I feel a bit guilty," Brett said quietly. "Sitting here when I should be figuring out who this Phil Arnold is – solving a murder."

"I just feel hungry," Clare replied. "It's a good menu in there. Even red snapper. Bit pricey, but good."

"Now you mention it..."

Clare interrupted him. "Look. Here we go," she whispered. "That's one of the assistants."

Outside, a furtive Lynne Freestone sidled into the restaurant.

"Well, well. Not Jordan Loveday or Huxford at all but the beady-eyed Lynne Freestone," Brett muttered. "Wait a bit," he said to Clare as the librarian took her place opposite Liz. "I want to know she's got that book with her before we move in. We'll just be able to see from here if and when she hands it over. Just hope that Liz has memorized her scholarly chat-up lines."

Inside, the two women were talking animately to each other.

"Wish I could lip-read," Clare said.

While Brett and Clare concentrated on the table in the window, another figure suddenly appeared in the restaurant doorway. In the restaurant, Liz swivelled in her seat and waved both palms madly on the other side of the glass. Her face was contorted by a grimace.

"Something's wrong!" Brett yelled. "Let's go!"

The man at the entrance was Mr Huxford. He was carrying a briefcase and as soon as he saw the two detectives he dashed down the street.

"Which one do we go for?" Clare queried.

"Huxford!" Brett decided. "Liz was trying to tell us it wasn't Lynne Freestone."

They sprinted along the road after the Head Librarian as Brett had done once before. This time, he was determined not to let Huxford escape. There weren't many people on the street. It was more of a flat race than an obstacle course but the pavement was still treacherous. At the first kerb, Clare was unable to control her speed and crashed heavily to the ground. Brett had no option but to leave her. He continued the pursuit. He knew that he was strong and fast enough to catch Huxford but he didn't know if the slippery surface would intervene, if the librarian would jump into a car and speed off, or if Huxford might give him the slip in a side-street.

They approached the end of the road, a T-junction. With relief, Brett saw a uniformed officer step out into Huxford's path. One of Liz's policemen, no doubt, stationed perfectly.

Sudden movements were impossible. Huxford slowed and slid to a halt. Brett also wound down to walking pace. Mr Huxford was sandwiched. He looked back at Brett and then forward to the policeman, trying to decide what to do. With the briefcase tucked under his right arm, he made off across the road – right in front of a bus. The driver panicked and braked hard. There was a loud squeal and the wheels of the bus locked. Its back wheels seemed to try to catch up with its front and it powered towards the end of the road almost sideways. Mr Huxford dived to one side as the bus skidded past him, hit the kerb, bounced into a parked car with a sickening crunch, and lurched alarmingly. The frightened passengers believed that the bus was about to fall on to its side. It was tottering like a drunk but when it finally toppled, it leant comically against a lamp-post and came to rest.

Brett left the bus to the policeman and looked round for Mr Huxford. He was hurrying back up the street on the opposite side. He was limping awkwardly. He must have hurt himself when he dodged the bus. Brett crossed the road when it was clear and followed the wounded man. By the time that Brett closed on him, he was near the restaurant again. He was weary and panting like a man who was not used to exercise.

Before Brett could grab him, Clare stepped out of a shop doorway and, in one easy movement, floored him. Professionally she clasped his hands securely behind him and pressed her knee into his back.

Huxford lay on the ground, incapacitated and helpless.

"Well done," Brett gasped. "Are you OK?"

"Yeah. Just a bruise. Still, it saved me the bother of a run."

"Let's open the bag, shall we?" Brett said, squatting down. Inside the black leather case there was a precious copy of the greatest scientific book ever written.

Above him, Lynne Freestone peered down and muttered, "Yes. That's it." Addressing her boss, she squawked, "How could you?"

Mr Huxford was saying nothing. He was too breathless and bewildered.

Brett stood up. "How come you're here?" he asked Lynne.

"I broke into Mr Loveday's E-mail to see if there was any evidence against him. I found your colleague's request and I intercepted the reply. I came here with a camera to trap Jordan Loveday in the act. I didn't for a moment think..."

She was so outraged by Mr Huxford's crime that she couldn't continue.

"It didn't occur to you that Mr Huxford had infiltrated Loveday's E-mail as well and was using it to conduct this little transaction," Brett deduced. "And to incriminate him even more." It was the second frame-up that Brett had witnessed in one day. First Stephanie Games, now Jordan Loveday. So much deceit!

The place was crawling with squad cars and police officers. Most were at the other end of the road, taking care of the bus passengers and keeping away sightseers. Brett said to Liz, "You did a good job. Huxford's all yours. Charge him but then get someone else to wrap it up, will you? We've got another case to think about. See you back at home base."

"Don't I even get a meal?" she replied with a grin.

Two uniformed officers dragged Mr Huxford to his feet and clung resolutely to each arm while Liz charged him with theft.

Brett and Clare returned to their car to find a parking ticket pinned to the windscreen by the wiper blade. "Efficient round here, aren't they?" Clare groaned.

When the team of three had reassembled at headquarters, Brett apologized to Liz. "I'm sorry to pull you back in but we've got a little mystery. I'll tell you what, though," Brett said, suddenly realizing how he could make it up to her, "I'll treat you to dinner at The Maltings if you can find me anything on someone called Phil Arnold."

"A meal on you? Right! You're on." She entered her computerized library of known and probable crooks. "Arnold," she murmured, tapping keys. "Phil." She waited for a few seconds and then sat back. "There you are. Hardly anything known about him, but he's there. Phil Arnold. Mine's the most expensive item on the menu, please."

Brett's face creased as he read the short entry. *Antivivisectionist. Member of the Campaign for Animal Rights. No known violent action. No objection to proposals for violent action.* "This," Brett declared, "must be from the police mole at CAR."

"Sounds like it," Clare agreed. "Not much detail."

"Liz," Brett said, "you've been hankering after a bit of glory. Here's your chance. Tomorrow you can arrest Hannah Farr for the murder of Colin Games. She probably got Dean to do her dirty work for her. That makes her just as guilty even if she can't face killing herself. She used Dean to swat the fly on her behalf."

"Another arrest? That's glory?" Liz retorted. "More like sweeping up after the party."

Brett continued, "That's not all. Question her about Phil Arnold. She's in CAR – perhaps she'll be able to lead us to him."

"OK," Liz replied. "But how many people are you going to arrest for one murder? Going for a world record?"

"Bit of a Julius Caesar job, this," Clare put in. "Everyone wanted to get their sword into him."

"While you hunt Phil Arnold through Hannah we'll do it through Paul Dunnett," Brett decided. "He's another CAR person. And I still want to question his assessment of Colin Games's chemistry skills."

"More importantly, when do I get my free meal?" Liz demanded.

"As soon as Phil Arnold confesses and shops the lot of them."

Behind Brett, the pale light cast on the wall of his front room rippled uncannily – a projection of movement in the aquarium. Brett had not switched on the main lamp. He stood in the window and watched the feathery snow falling inexhaustibly. It drifted down, unhurried and hypnotic, like reflective confetti against a black curtain. When each sliver of ice touched the lawn, it added infinitesimally to the city's white cloak. Together, though, the countless snowflakes made a lavish covering. Tomorrow would be a day of loud groans, whoops of delight, closed schools, blocked roads, chaos and snowmen. Brett hoped that it would also be a day of resolution. He turned away from the window, drained his glass of scotch, and got ready for bed.

In the morning the world looked as if it had been

bleached. As Brett jogged through the park, his trainers scrunched through the snow satisfyingly. He felt much more in control than over the past few frosty days. The compression of the snow provided grip. Ironically, the luxurious layer invited a playful tumble. It offered a cotton-wool landing and a refreshing roll. Brett resisted the temptation. But he understood the Inuits' need for different labels for different snows. This version was pure and attractive. So unlike the slippery, slushy stuff. The two forms of the same substance deserved two different names – the Jekyll and Hyde of snow. Running seemed easy and immensely pleasurable, so Brett accelerated. His thoughts turned to another Jekyll and Hyde character: Mr Huxford, the pleasant and polite Head Librarian, and Mr Huxford, the greedy and deceitful thief who had pretended to be Jordan Loveday. Another double life. Brett couldn't remember who was the goody in the novel – Jekyll or Hyde. He could recall only that, in the film, the good one was handsome, upright and well-dressed. When he transformed into a baddie, he became ugly, bent and squalid. Brett smiled at the notion. It would make his job a lot easier if it happened like that in real life.

When he got back home, he felt stretched, slightly breathless and ready to take on the world. He showered, ate a simple breakfast, and glanced at a newspaper while he waited for his partner to arrive like a chauffeur.

On the way to the interview with Dr Dunnett, Liz radioed. "This morning," she informed him, "you got a message from on high. The Chief wants a progress report. He wants progress. Otherwise, he said he's going to pull me off the case. Sounded a bit miffed. But I … er … reassured him."

"What did you say?" Brett asked.

"I told him we'd already charged Dean Games, that I'm about to arrest Hannah Farr, and that you've been filling up the cells with lots of suspects. But the real problem is that he wanted to know why we'd been involved in a case of book theft and why we tried to kill a busload of Sheffield citizens."

"Ah," Brett murmured. "He's heard. Did you reassure him on that one as well?"

"I did my best," Liz replied. "He might be under the impression that we went to The Maltings to meet Jordan Loveday and interview him about the murder. Because of his connection with Hannah Farr. He might be under the impression that the rest happened by chance. But you're supposed to be creative, Brett," she chirped. "I'm sure your report'll back up what I said. Besides, it was the only way to save your skin."

Brett smiled ruefully. "Thanks, I think."

Before they reached Xenox, Brett said, "Hey, Clare. You're into literature. Who was the goody – Jekyll or Hyde?"

Clare grinned. "The good Dr Jekyll transformed into the evil Mr Hyde. An allegory, they say, for the struggle between the good and evil in every one of us. Perhaps," she contemplated with a grin, "it suggests doctors can't be baddies because he lost his title when he took on his evil persona. Why?"

"Oh, I was just thinking. This morning when I was running. I was thinking of Huxford, mainly."

"Heavyweight kind of thoughts for that early," she commented. "Me, I stumble around, restricting myself to finding a toothbrush, toaster, clothes and coffee."

Brett chuckled. He could not imagine his partner stumbling around. She had the admirable elegance and practised poise of a martial-arts disciple.

Clare drove carefully. Where the authorities had not cleared the roads, the tyres crunched on snow and compacted it. No problem for Clare and Brett but, for the cars behind, it left a slick, hardened surface like ice. The streets were not as busy as usual. Several people must have got up, looked out on to the Scandinavian landscape, given up and gone back to their nice warm beds. On the pavements, half of the children carried school bags and the other half carried sledges. The car park at Xenox was not full by any means. Clearly, several workers had not made it into work. The open spaces in the car park contained tyre tracks making weird and wonderful looping patterns like a well-used skating rink.

The security station was besieged by the cold. The officers were clapping their hands to keep warm. One of them recognized Brett and Clare, saying, "Is it Dr Dunnett you want again?"

"Yes. Is he in today?"

"Yes. He's one who gets in, come what may. The rest of his staff haven't arrived yet, but I'll call and check if he'll see you."

The guard had to call three different numbers before he located Paul Dunnett in one of the laboratories. "Apparently," the security officer said after he put down the phone, "he's in a bit of a panic, trying to run the department on his own. He can't leave the lab but he'll see you there, where he can carry on with some tests while he speaks to you. I'm to take you directly to the laboratory. This way, please."

The laboratory occupied the whole of one side of the building. Long and narrow, it was divided into different sections, each with their own doors into the main corridor. There were units dedicated to computer analysis of data, separation of mixtures using exotic instrumentation, structure analysis. Some of the instruments had pumps that chugged gently or fans that whirred. Somewhere a neglected computer bleeped for attention like a duckling that had lost its mother. There were rows of chemicals in dark bottles, fire extinguishers and even a shower for dousing personnel who had become contaminated with dangerous materials. Stickers on the walls warned people with pacemakers not to enter certain parts of the lab because of the strong magnetic field. It would also wipe clean any credit cards, according to the notice. One cupboard bore a skull and cross-bones, another carried a biohazard caution and a third was blessed with a gruesome sign showing a hand with a bit missing. Underneath, the notice warned of corrosive liquids. Clare shivered. Unlike Brett, she was not in her element. To her, the laboratory seemed scary because it was so alien. This time, there was no Derek Jacob to make her feel comfortable.

Paul Dunnett was dressed in a white lab coat and safety spectacles. He wore bright blue gloves as he transferred some liquids from beakers into vials on a carousel using a syringe. He glanced behind him at his visitors. "With you in a few seconds," he announced.

"I'll leave you to it," the security guard boomed and then left.

Dunnett stood up, coughed and murmured, "That's it." He walked a few steps to a computer and gave the instruction to start the procedure. "I can't leave for a bit," he told them. "I need to make sure everything's OK before I let it get on with the analysis itself. But I'm happy to talk here." A robotic arm swung over the carousel and reached down for one of the sample vials. Hesitatingly, it lifted the vial towards the inlet of the instrument.

"It's only a couple of questions," Brett began. "A couple of simple things you can clear up. You see, we spoke to Colin Games's old tutor at York, Roger Bassindale. Your supervisor as well, I gather. Anyway, he seemed less than enthusiastic about Colin's science skills. You were very complimentary, though. Big difference," Brett remarked.

Paul took off his safety glasses and shrugged. "Just different perceptions of him, I guess." He shifted uneasily.

"But didn't he just copy all your work at York?"

"Maybe he was a late developer," Paul replied, the agitation clear in his tone.

Brett realized that he had uncovered a contentious issue and decided to pursue it further. He hoped to provoke Dunnett into an outburst that would reveal all. "I gather that all Colin's best ideas really came from you."

"Look," Paul snapped, "I don't know why you're labouring this thing. Can't we drop it?"

"When I understand it, yes," Brett replied. "*Did* he get all his ideas from you and copy your work?"

Suddenly, the robotic arm jerked into action and removed the first vial. Putting it back in its place in the carousel, it paused and then faltered towards the next sample.

"Not all of it," Paul said. "But it's a very sore point." He sniffed and then cleared his throat.

"So, why did you insist he was so bright?"

Dunnett's eyes displayed unrestrained irritation. "It's called fibbing, Lawless. You obviously thought he'd been murdered so I didn't want to tell you I had a grudge against him. I didn't want to admit to a motive. No doubt PHP told you he was good as well.

After all, he got them their cure for baldness. That's all they cared about. They equate genius with profit. But he must have hit upon it by sheer accident."

Brett hesitated. "This is all about his baldness drug, isn't it?" he surmised.

"All those years at university I gave him his best ideas – and he always 'borrowed' my course work before he completed his own," Paul grumbled fiercely. "Then he stumbled across a new drug and he wouldn't share it with me like I used to share my work with him. It should've been my pay-off time but he turned his back on me. That's the sore point."

"I see," Brett muttered thoughtfully. Changing direction, he asked, "Do you know Phil Arnold? Another CAR member?"

Paul's mouth opened but for a second nothing emerged. In that moment, Brett knew the answer to his question. He did not need Dunnett's response. Brett had discovered another Jekyll and Hyde character. More duplicity. The good Dr Dunnett had transformed into the evil Mr Arnold. Brett glanced at Clare, and from her expression, he realized that she had also figured it out. To Simon Mortimer, the chemist from Xenox was Paul Dunnett. He had to be, because Mortimer knew him at Yorkshire Water. To Hannah and Dean, he was Phil Arnold. As a spy, he'd joined CAR under a different name. If he'd used his real name, CAR would have researched his background and discovered that he was from Xenox. Brett murmured, "You're Phil Arnold! Of course you'd use a false name when you infiltrated CAR. Hannah knew you by your alias."

Abruptly, Dunnett made a run for it. He weaved round an instrument and made for a door further down the lab. Brett followed him but Clare, thinking quickly, took a different route. She went out of the nearest door and, without the obstacles of laboratory furniture, hurtled down the corridor towards the next door. She hoped to reach it before Dunnett.

Inside, Brett sent a tray of samples scattering across the floor as he brushed past a bench. His speed didn't help here. It was all about agility and knowledge of the laboratory layout. Dunnett was getting away from him. Just as the murderer reached the final cupboard before the exit, Clare burst in through the door. All three of them halted, uncertain. Dunnett was trapped between Clare and Brett.

Clare was closer and walked towards him. "Paul Dunnett," she proclaimed. "We're arresting you for..."

With his bright blue and protected hands, Dunnett reached into the nearest fume cupboard and drew out a large beaker of smoking yellow liquid. He clasped it in his right hand, ready to throw the contents at Clare.

She took another step nearer to him.

"No!" Brett yelled at her. "Don't try anything."

"Wise words," Dunnett mocked. "You know what this is, don't you, Lawless?"

The fume cupboard bore the silhouette of the decomposing hand. "I recognize this type of lab," Brett replied, horrified at what Dunnett was threatening to do. "It's where you destroy organic matter ready for elemental analysis. You've got concentrated acid."

"The most corrosive cocktail of acids we've got. Digests anything." To Clare, he snarled, "Goes through clothes and skin like a flame through wax. Very nice. So just back off!"

"Do what he says, Clare," Brett advised her. Trying to warn her not to kick her way out of it this time, he said, "This isn't like a knife. It'll go everywhere."

She took a few paces back but still blocked the door.

Caught between them with no way out, Dunnett cried, "Back off!"

"It's no use," Brett told him. Coming closer to the chemist, he said, "We know. Even if you get out of this lab, we'll be after you."

"Don't push your luck," Dunnet growled.

Gathering her wits and trying to encourage him to talk, Clare said, "You killed Games because he refused to tell you the identity of his drug. Is that it?"

Wild, but still willing to defame his old university colleague, Paul hissed, "More than that. He refused to have anything to do with me. He even tried to tell me *I'd* copied *him* at York." Dunnett snorted disdainfully. "He only got that job at PHP because I dragged him through university. When they showered him with money he turned his back on me."

"So, you wanted revenge," Clare deduced. "That's what anyone would want in your place." She watched him carefully. There was a lot of liquid in the beaker. No doubt it was heavy. She'd noticed that his right arm was slowly sagging under the weight. She hoped to keep him talking until he couldn't hold it any more. She wanted to provoke a conversation but she could not risk aggravating him. She wanted him to spill words, not acid.

"I worked out how to do something about it. It was easy. I used to know Simon Mortimer. Before coming here I worked in the analytical section at Yorkshire Water. Our paths crossed there. I got in touch with him again, wondering how he was enjoying working with the self-styled great man." He spat out irony. "Mortimer wasn't, of course. No one could enjoy working with *that*. So, we hatched a plan."

Realizing his partner's tactics, Brett joined in. "And you couldn't get the drug structure from Simon because Games kept it to himself."

"That wasn't the issue any more. It was Games's selfishness. His spite. His twisting the truth. Trying to play the role of Nobel-prize winner when he was useless. That's what I had to stop. At first, the plan lacked one thing. A good way of feeding heavy water to him over a few weeks. Simon could have arranged something at PHP – at break times – but my calculations showed it wasn't enough. We needed to recruit someone closer to him. His wife was an unknown quantity but I bumped into someone who could help. Courtesy of the Campaign for Animal Rights. I've got no sympathy with CAR – none at all – but my boss here asked me to pretend to sympathize, to go to CAR meetings undercover. CAR was planning a campaign against PHP, Xenox and people like us. The boss wanted to know if they were planning any direct action against Xenox. The answer was no, but I found out something much more valuable. I came across Hannah Farr, a CAR activist with the job of infiltrating the Games household. She was leading Dean Games by the nose, and I found out from her that Dean wasn't exactly enamoured of his father. Unfortunately, she'd already sent some sort of threatening letter to Games but I reckoned it hadn't queered my pitch too much."

"Does Hannah have any real feelings for Dean," Clare interjected glumly, "or is she just doing a job for CAR?"

"Oh, she has real feelings all right," Dunnett replied with a nasty sneer. "She despises him as much as I despise his rotten father. It was a good partnership. And such a waste to have only one person exploiting the gullible Dean, so I muscled in on the act as well, with Hannah's blessing. Dean wanted his dad's money to spend on her and Hannah was pushing him to help her – and CAR – exact revenge on the family for its work with animals. So you see, it was a joint effort. Mutual benefit."

Behind Clare a piercing beep sounded and she jumped nervously.

Paul chuckled insanely. "Just a computer telling me it's ready for the next batch of samples."

Clare breathed again.

"Why use heavy water?" Brett enquired.

Paul adjusted his grip on the flask of acid and lifted it slightly, trying to resuscitate his tired arm. "First, we wanted to see him suffer. But why stop there? It was an ideal opportunity to get rid of him altogether. We used heavy water because we expected his death would go down as a mystery." Momentarily, Dunnett peered at Brett with hate in his eyes. "We didn't know we'd be lumbered with a cop who knows his science. But with heavy water, we could arrange it that, if the murder *was* discovered, we could frame his wife. We knew from Dean that she had a lover, so she had a motive. She knew enough biochemistry and she had plenty of opportunity to poison him."

"I suppose it was your calculations that allowed Dean to make himself slightly sick with heavy water without doing any real, lasting damage," Brett inferred.

"Nice touch, I thought," Paul smirked. He sneezed violently but kept hold of the precious, menacing beaker. "Just in case you got anywhere, Dean 'volunteered' to make himself ill. Once it was obvious you were on to the heavy water – when you interviewed Simon at work – Simon phoned Dean straightaway. Arranged to give him some more to plant at his house that evening."

"I guess he also arranged for Hannah to come and see us to reinforce the notion of her boyfriend's failing health." Brett shook his head slowly. "Didn't work." He continued, "Ashton wasn't so much a lover as a plaything. Nothing to commit murder over. Besides, Stephanie Games hadn't really got the means to get all that heavy water away from PHP."

Dunnett rested the heavy beaker on the lip of the cupboard but maintained his grasp and his vigilance. "Pity," he murmured.

"Why did Mortimer provide the heavy water, not you?" Brett queried.

"I could've done it, but I might've got caught. I persuaded Mortimer to do it instead. There's no gain, I told him, without risk." Paul grinned proudly. "He intercepted the orders before they got to the analytical section. When you're as tall as him, it's amazing what you can hide inside a big winter coat. Easy. One bottle at a time. He only had to get each one as far as his car and he was clean away with it. A heavy coat for heavy water," Paul quipped. "He soon built up a stockpile at home. Anyway," he murmured, banishing his crazy smile, "enough of our cosy chat. Time you stood aside."

"We can't do that, Paul," Clare stated. "It's time you let go of the acid. Leave it there, step away from it and let's end it now. You don't want anything else against you. Judges are never lenient on people who have a go at the arresting officer."

Paul made no attempt to surrender. "No chance!" he uttered. "Unless you hadn't noticed, *I'm* in control here."

He sounded exactly like Jordan Loveday last Sunday. This time, though, Clare was faced with an unfamiliar weapon. She knew how to disarm crooks with guns, sticks, knives. She could turn the strength of unarmed opponents against themselves. But there had been no training for dealing with fuming acids. It was an insidious, frightening weapon. It would not kill, she guessed, but it would disfigure and blind. Finally, she had met a weapon that appalled her more than knives. "We've already got Simon, Dean and Hannah in custody," she said. "It's all over."

"Not while I'm holding this," he retorted, glancing down at the acid. "Now, move away from the door," he ordered her.

Clare looked at Brett and saw him nod. His lips mouthed, "No choice."

"All right," she said regretfully. "I'm backing away."

Dunnett glanced over his shoulder at Brett and muttered, "You won't do anything rash. You know the potency of this stuff." He turned his back on Brett.

Paul Dunnett was right. Brett was helpless. But he remembered his Chief's words. "You'll virtually be on home territory." Brett looked round the lab for inspiration.

Clare took two steps backwards and her elbow caught a warm flask that was perched on top of a hot plate. The vessel fell, spewing its liquid contents over the bench. The clear fluid splashed, spread over the surface of the bench and dribbled over the edge. Some of it spattered on to Clare's sleeve and she let out a small, involuntary shriek. The glass flask rolled off the bench and smashed on the floor.

Paul laughed at her distress. "You'll live," he cackled. "It's a solvent mixture. Water with a bit of alcohol. That's all. A bit like spilling vodka."

Clare exhaled and then breathed in deeply, composing herself again. She wasn't on the edge of panic but she was hardly relaxed. The unfamiliar terrain did not put her at ease. To Clare the laboratory was like a jungle with fearsome creatures lurking unseen behind each bench. She sighed. Two more steps back and she would clear Paul's way to the exit.

From beyond the door, there was the sound of footsteps. Someone was walking down the corridor. Dunnett put the blue forefinger of his left hand to his lips and remained still. Half a minute later, the footfalls receded. Dunnett looked behind him and then exclaimed, "Where's Lawless? He's gone."

Clare shrugged. She really didn't know. He had disappeared from view when they'd been diverted by the broken flask and the spillage.

Dunnett spun round and yelled down the length of the laboratory. "Come out, Lawless!" Petulant and neurotic, he cried, "Come out or she gets it!"

Clare could have flattened him easily in those few seconds when his back was turned but Brett had alerted her to the danger. The vile liquid in Dunnett's hand could fly anywhere if she went on the offensive. The fact that Brett had ducked out of sight told her that he had a plan of his own. He knew laboratories and he knew about acids. Surely he's got a plan, she prayed, trying to convince and comfort herself. This time, she would leave it to him. Her intuition told her to put some distance between herself and Paul Dunnett, even if it meant giving him free access to the door. If Brett was about to strike, she needed to be as far away as possible from the threat of the acid. Glancing behind her to make sure she didn't knock over anything else, she began to tiptoe backwards.

"I'm warning you, Lawless!" Dunnett shouted again. His voice was increasingly crazed. "Show yourself!"

"All right," Brett called back from behind one of the large instruments. "I'm coming out." For a few more seconds, though, he delayed, remaining hidden.

Clearly, he was giving Clare as much time as he could. She continued to retreat quietly.

Suddenly, Brett emerged into the open. In his hand was a fire hose. He opened the tap and a powerful jet of water sprayed from the nozzle. He directed the torrent at Dunnett, aiming particularly for the beaker of acid.

In an instant, Dunnett was drenched. The force of the stream blasted the beaker out of his hand. As it scuttled across the floor, Brett played the gushing water on to it, converting concentrated acid to harmless, dilute acid.

Some of the spurting water splashed around the lab. Behind Dunnett, Clare was also caught in the deluge. She leapt in the air as the beaker skidded past her feet. To Dunnett's left, an electronic box was soaked. It gave out a flash and exploded. It acted like a starting gun. Dunnett made a dive for Brett. He was no match, though, for the surge from the hose. Brett played the stream on to his chest and it checked him.

Losing his footing, Dunnett fell backwards and landed on the slippery floor with a splash. Saturated and exhausted, he ended up at Clare's feet. Clare dropped on him and pinned him to the ground. "OK, OK!" she screamed at Brett who continued to play the water over both of them. "Enough!" she shouted. "I've got him."

"Did you get acid on you anywhere?" Brett asked urgently. "Any itches or pain? Any on your legs?"

Just in case, he doused her legs before shutting off the valve.

Clare blew the moisture away from her mouth and shook her head free of drops. All of her clothes clung icily and uncomfortably to her skin. Her fine, red hair was plastered unflatteringly to her head. She cursed and grumbled, "You really know how to give a woman a good time, don't you? Where did they teach you that trick? It's the coldest, wettest, worst shower I've ever had."

"Sorry," Brett said with a relieved smile. "But there are worse things to be showered with." Still holding the fire hose but talking to Dunnett, he asked, "Did any of the acid get on you?"

He did not answer. Paul Dunnett had lapsed into stunned silence.

Brett put down the hose pipe and examined the chemist's arms. His gloves had protected his hands from the spilt acid and his lab coat had charred in places but it had done its job. None of the corrosive liquid had penetrated to his skin. "You're OK," Brett concluded. "Let's get you up."

Together they yanked the sodden and docile murderer to his feet. Supported, he stood and dripped pathetically like a drowned rat. "As my partner was saying," Brett said into his ear, "we're going to charge you with the murder of Colin Games. First, we're taking you in. The doctor'll need to look you over and make sure you're fit to understand what's going on."

"Before that, Brett," Clare put in, "I could use a towel. I'm freezing!"

What had started with water had ended with water.

Independently, Hannah and Dean identified Paul Dunnett as the man that they knew as Phil Arnold: the bandleader of the cold-blooded quartet. By the end of the day, Brett had wrapped up the case with four confessions, Clare was snivelling – the first ominous signs of a cold – and Liz was straining at the leash for her free meal.

"I've got a report to write," Brett grumbled. "And, in places, it requires a little imagination."

"You can do the paperwork tomorrow," Liz said. "I'll even help – a bit. Clare can stay at home and take hot baths and aspirin. Right now, I hear The Maltings calling."

Brett relented. He treated both Liz and Clare. It cost him a fortune but he had to repay the expertise and hard work that Liz had brought to the case and he had to make up for giving Clare an unwanted, freezing shower. In the restaurant, he didn't even complain when his partners both ordered red snapper.

On Wednesday, he had two calls from the university. First, the secretary of the disciplinary committee wanted official confirmation of the charge against their Head Librarian and the innocence of Jordan Loveday. Then, an hour later, he had Jordan himself on the line. "I just wanted to thank you," he said. "I'm back in favour with the university. Even got myself an apology. I can put it all behind me now."

Brett sighed. "Not quite, I'm afraid. There's still the matter of threatening behaviour and possession of an offensive weapon."

"I suppose so," Jordan admitted. "What's going to happen to me?"

Brett told him, "You can't go around waving knives at people, especially when they're police officers. But..." He hesitated and then said, "I shouldn't say this, but a word in the right ear might help. You were obviously provoked to a considerable extent. My guess is, you'll be convicted but given a suspended sentence because of the mitigating circumstances. It means you'll be able to keep up your studies. Back on track."

"Thanks," he repeated, a little wearily but no longer fearful. "I want you to know I appreciate it. I really didn't think you'd bother with me."

Brett smiled to himself and murmured, "I was a student once."

Later, standing in front of Keith Johnstone, he explained Clare's absence. Exaggerating to try and win her more sympathy, he said, "Bad case of flu, sir."

"Flu, eh?" The Chief waved Brett's report and replied, "I see how she got it." More sombre, he said, "And I *can* read between the lines, you know. Much as you've tried to hide it. When I put you on a case, Brett, I expect you to keep to it. Especially when you twist my arm for more resources. I don't expect you to get drawn into every passing case of litter dropping, handbag snatching, and dogs leaving unpleasant surprises in the park," he admonished. "All right?"

Brett nodded. "Yes, sir."

"OK. Otherwise, it was a job extremely well done. Because of that, I'm not going to throw the book at you. Valuable or not." He chuckled at his own pun.

Brett wanted to cringe at the joke, but smiled politely instead.

Clearly in a good mood because a major crime had been solved in under two weeks with the minimum of officers, Keith added, "Just play it by the book next time."

Brett allowed the smile on his face to linger as long as possible to humour the Chief.

"And talking of next time," Keith said, "I've just received notice of another funny one. A body on the outskirts of Worksop with a calling card pinned to it." Looking at his computer screen, he continued, "The message was, *You'll be getting to know me*. That's all. Sounds weird. Sounds like one of yours. You seem to thrive on them. I'm putting you and Clare in charge of it. You'd better get out there right away. If Clare's had the day off, she'll be as right as rain tomorrow. It's only flu, after all. She can start first thing in the morning."

Look out for the first

It's not for the faint-hearted.

The Secrets of the Dead

THE CASE: Four bodies have been found in the Peak District. They're rotting fast and vital evidence needs to be taken from the corpses. You need a strong stomach to work in Forensics...

Brett's got a theory, but it could cost him his job. He's going to pursue it anyway...

The third Lawless & Tilley is coming soon:
MAGIC EYE
It's an enigma.